the DEVIL in DISGUISE

MAYA DANIELS

VINCI
BOOKS

The
DEVIL
in
DISGUISE

MAYA DANIELS

VINCI
BOOKS

By Maya Daniels

The Broken Halos Series

The Devil is in the Details
Speak of the Devil
Encounter with the Devil
The Devil in Disguise
To Look the Devil in the Eye
Better the Devil You Know
Give a Devil His Due

Vinci Books

vinci-books.com

Published by Vinci Books Ltd in 2025

1

A CIP catalogue record for this book is available from the British Library.

Paperback ISBN: 9781036706623

The EU GPSR authorised representative is Logos Europe, 9 rue Nicolas Poussion, 17000 La Rochelle, France contact@logoseurope.eu

Chapter One

HELENA

Assholes!

I'm surrounded by men that are complete idiots, and cavemen. All my worries about making the biggest mistake that humankind has ever made are erased within thirty minutes of walking out through the portal. I'm even debating if staying in Hell and dealing with Mammon and his horde of demons might be a better option.

I found my home in flames, and it wasn't just Atlanta burning, no. The whole world is in shambles, the demons taking dominion over everything. I stood there, my mouth hanging open in utter disbelief as I wondered, okay hoped, that we took a wrong turn in the portal and we are back in Hell.

We are not.

There is no sign of Maddison, or Raphael either. For two days we've been lurking in the shadows, trying to locate them. Only we've had no luck. At that point, Colt, Beelzebub, my sidekick Narsi, and Leviathan decided to proclaim themselves my protectors. My keepers, more like it. Overbearing, bullheaded, stubborn assholes is what I call them. My worries about humans and what will happen to them were for nothing because the three men don't plan on taking over and destroying them. Instead, they took over my life and are killing my sanity with every passing minute I spend with them.

The building where Maddison's office was hidden with wards is no longer standing. A crater as big as an entire block was what stared me in the face when I lead my band of jerks there. Next stop was the demon sanctuary, which was nothing but a junkyard again. Not a soul stirred, and there were no clues left behind for me to find.

So, here we are in Eric's penthouse, where the front door has been ripped open and the pristine furniture, along with the paintings, have been shattered into tiny pieces and thrown around the main room. They didn't just search for whatever they were looking for. It looks like someone had a fit of rage, and since they couldn't get their hands on him, they took it out on everything else but the walls.

Maybe they wanted to get their hands on you. The voice in my head points out, sending a shiver down my spine.

Anger mixes with my trepidation of what has happened in my absence from the human realm. The empty building shudders, brick and mortar groaning when the ground shakes under us. The Trowe whimpers, clutching at my arm.

"She's getting angry again." The urgency in Colt's voice pisses me off even more.

"Calm down, Helena." Beelzebub pets me awkwardly on the head.

"Stop touching me, damn it!" Snarling at him, I shove his hand away, and Narsi bares his yellowed teeth at him. He is cool like that.

We've been sitting in the dark, destroyed penthouse for a couple of hours now trying to come up with a plan on what to do next. Beelzebub places Eric on top of the shredded fabric we gathered, creating a makeshift mattress. The wound on my mate's ribs is still open, but Leviathan did some juju, and at least the blood is not flowing from it anymore. The fact that he is not healing but looks like he is sleeping is coiling dread in my chest. Eric should've been awake, or at least fully recovered by now.

"It won't help if you bring the building down on our heads, girl. Control yourself!" Leviathan snaps at me, shocking me into silence. "We have other things to worry about instead of reminding you to calm down every five minutes."

"Listen to me you jerk!" Shaking off the stunned stare he turns at me, I glare at him. "This might be an okay situation in your demonic head." Sweeping my arm around, I point out the chaos. "But it does not sit well with me. While I was stuck in Hell, playing your twisted games, look what happened to my world. And it's all because of me."

"You should stop feeling sorry for yourself. If it weren't you, it would've been someone else." The Viking-looking fallen stares down his nose at me. "This was inevitable and a long time coming. It's on us that we looked the other way while Mammon had his temper tantrums."

My fingers twitch with the need to stick the pointy bit of my dagger in his forehead. "So, what you're saying is Lucifer knew this was about to happen, he just didn't think it was worth his time to stop it?"

"If my father knew, then Michael would've as well," Colt pipes in defensively.

"What, they are buddies now?" Narrowing my gaze at Colt, I watch him squirm, probably thinking I'll jump and attack him. I might be getting a little unhinged, but I don't have the time to worry about me right now. "Last time I saw the Holy ass, he was hell bent on killing Lucifer."

"We are not sure that it was Michael," Beelzebub states, exposing the obvious elephant in the room.

And there it is. The biggest of our problems. We have no idea who is who, if we have spoken to the real people or a motherfucking jinn disguising as them. It's all a cluster-fuck, and I'm the point zero, the center, of it all. Maybe if I let them kill me, things will get back to normal. They won't. I just like to have morose thoughts floating through my head right now.

"I can't sit around and wait for a bright idea to strike me on what our next move should be. I need to do something." I need to hunt some jinn is more like it, but I don't say that out loud.

"We can go to that Sanctuary you told us about," Colt says helpfully. "Maybe we can find some clues there."

"I will go to see if I can find someone willing to shed some light on the situation." Leviathan stretches his muscly arms over his head. "I'll meet you back here when I'm done."

"Not as a freaking dragon!"

Oops. I might've shouted louder than I should've.

The last thing I need is everyone seeing a dragon with hellfire down its spine right now. I know without seeing any humans around that they are freaked out of their minds. The Order protected them from things they shouldn't be seeing, or even know about. Now, nothing is standing between them and their worst nightmares.

"Not as a dragon, no," Leviathan smirks at me, and I do throw a piece of broken furniture at his head.

A wooden leg, I think from one of the sofas, sails

through the air but the fallen moves too fast, ducks, and the wood bounces off the wall behind him, falling with a thud. Beelzebub chuckles, shaking his head, amusement dancing in his eyes. Shrugging a shoulder, I ignore the death glare from Leviathan.

"Well, go on then, dragon boy." Shooing him with my hand, I bare my teeth at him like a deranged person. "Go fetch."

The hairs on the back of my neck stand on end when a feral growl rumbles from Leviathan's chest. The icy-blue eyes, cold as a glacier, glare at me, and I give him the sweetest smile. Even Colt laughs at this, angering the fallen angel more. I either really have a death wish, or I'm confident that he won't hurt me. It's an unsettling thought, so I push it with the rest of the things I've become good at ignoring. Turning on his heels, Leviathan storms out of the apartment. Luckily, the door is still hanging askew, or I'm sure he would've slammed it when making his exit.

"You shouldn't antagonize him that much, Helena." Beelzebub chuckles again. "I don't think the old man has dealt with females from this time. It's a very big adjustment for him."

"Do you know how many fucks I have to give for his adjustment right now?" Petting my pockets, I blink at Beelzebub innocently. "None. I have no fucks left."

Colt roars with laughter and Beelzebub, throwing his head back, joins him. Even Narsi snickers creepily from next to me. My lips twitch, but that's all I manage when my eyes fall on Eric's sleeping form. Reaching my hand out, I glide my fingers over his good wing, the feathers soft on my skin. *Wake up, please*, I urge him with everything in me. Only the slow lifting of his chest keeps me from breaking down into a sobbing mess.

I can't do this without him.

He can be annoying, overprotective, and everything else that he is, but he's also the only thing keeping me fighting for my life and not giving up. When the world tilted under my feet, it was him that grabbed my hand and never let go. I need to find answers. If not for myself than for Eric. He almost got himself killed to protect me.

And I will kill to wake him up.

The thought is a very sobering one, and I blink fast, pulling myself out of the dark ideas swirling through my mind. Sitting around won't solve anything. As much as I like to hide here in hopes everything will go away or sort itself out, I know it won't.

They want me.

I'll just make sure my dagger is shoved between their ribs before they get a chance to strike. Turning around, I search the solemn faces of Colt and Beelzebub, ignoring the weird purring sound from my sidekick. They watch me warily, and I'm grateful there is no pity in their eyes.

"Let's go." Lifting myself off the floor, I don't wait for them. "Narsi, you stay and guard Eric. If one feather is missing from him, I'm going to skin you alive." Heading for the door, I only pause for a second when Colt speaks.

"Where are you going?"

"To find Raphael." I continue walking without turning to look if they will follow. "The Archangel has a lot of explaining to do."

Chapter Two

HELENA

Slinking through the streets of my city like a thief, I push away the GPS that is blaring alarms in my head, destructing me. I used to hate the gut feeling because it made me so giddy, and because it only came on during hunts. Now, while I hide like I don't belong in my own world, the anxiety and giddiness that accompanies it is a constant reminder that I shouldn't bitch about things, because they can always get worse.

Plastering myself to the wall of the Bank of America, it's building broken in half and sticking in the air like a shard of glass, I blow breath through pursed lips. My heart is jackhammering in my rib cage, every thump painful like it's trying to break free. Across the street, a massive billboard with two cows painting the words "Eat more chicken" is like a painful reminder of the dream I had the day my life went to shit.

Memories of me running through the deserted streets of Atlanta with Michael hot on my heels while Eric was trying to wake me up push to the front of my mind. Was that some sort of premonition, telling me what was on its way? Did I miss the significance of it, assuming the Holy ass was simply trying to murder me in my sleep? My dreams have always been messed up, showing me things in a mirror image. If I dreamed about something good happening, the opposite would happen in real life. Was that what that nightmare was? Because here I am, in the empty streets of Atlanta, running around while I'm desperate for Eric to wake up.

A crunch of gravel and the rustling of fabric yanks me out of my head. Jerking my head to the right, I see Colt gliding towards me, Beelzebub not far behind him. So, they decided to come along. Oh, the joy! A giddy feeling stirs in my belly when Colt's face gets partially illuminated by the street lights. My heart leaps in my throat, the stupid organ not realizing that it's not Eric. They look exactly the same. Physically at least, and only in their human form. I have no clue what my face displays because Colt's eyes soften when he stops next to me. I scowl at him, not wanting his sympathy.

I want blood.

Beelzebub walks by me, his body brushing mine when he sticks his head out to survey our surroundings. I know the moment he sees the group of demons from the ilk of Abaddon, who are gathered a few buildings down from where we are hiding. His body stiffens, a muscle jumping in his jaw.

"There are five of them." Looking over his shoulder at Colt, something passes between them that I'm apparently not privy to.

Colt nods, turning around and disappearing in the shadows. In my head, since I obviously haven't come to terms with the fact that demons are not mindless creatures that only like to eat and rip apart humans, I still expect them to plow blindly into a fray, horns, and claws lashing out. Their powers are overwhelming, the status of being Archdemons and Princes of Hell evident to anyone in their proximity, so to me, they seem untouchable. Eric's sleeping face reminds me of how stupid that thought is. So, they do think strategically and look for ways to come out on top in every situation because they can get hurt, or killed, just like anyone else. It makes me feel better about myself.

Yeah, I know. I've become petty like that.

"Stay here," Beelzebub looks down at me, his eyes glinting like flames on his handsome face. "We will get rid of them, then we will continue to your Sanctuary."

"How noble of you, asshole." Shouldering away from his overwhelming presence, I ignore the growl coming from his chest. "If you think I'll sit here like a scared little girl while the two of you fight my battles, you'll be sorely disappointed. This is my city, and you are only visiting, for now. As soon as this shit is over, your asses are going back to Hell if it's the last thing I do." Locking my gaze with his, even though my neck hurts because I have to look up, I make sure he sees how serious I am. "Every chance I get to kill one of those motherfuckers, I'm taking it. If you stand in my way, you might just end up with my dagger in your chest."

"Easy there." Lifting both hands in surrender, he eyes my fingers, which are grazing the hilt of my dagger, warily. "We need you alive and not bleeding all over the place. There is enough of them here already to deal with, so there's no need to open another portal for Mammon to send more."

Okay, so he has a point, but I'll die before I tell him that he is right. I can't sit back and watch while everything is falling apart. Flaring my nostrils, I take a deep breath, still unwilling to accept his reasonable words.

"I don't have to go first." Acting like I'm doing him a solid by letting him join me, I shrug. "I can follow behind and get the strays trying to get away from the two of you." Poking him with a finger in his firm chest, my lips press in a thin line. "But I'm not hiding while they terrorize my world."

Beelzebub searches my face for a long moment, those phantom-less eyes staring right into my soul. A shiver crawls up and down my spine, but I don't look away. I'm surrounded by predators, and the second I yield to their stubborn ass, they'll walk all over me. Like hell, I'll let that happen.

"You stay behind me." His voice is firm and breaks no argument.

"Yeah, sure." Shrugging both shoulders slightly, I pull out my dagger. "Lead the way, oh great one, and I shall follow in your shadow."

He shakes his head at my antics, rubbing his forehead as if I'm giving him a headache. It makes me miss Eric more because even when he is an overprotective jerk, he never rolls his eyes at me or makes me feel like I'm a hassle. The fact that he might've been an enabler, allowing me to have my temper tantrums and act on impulse—which might have been what led us all the way to hell— is not important. I miss his annoying ass.

Something powerful and dark stirs in my chest, taking me by surprise. Staggering on my feet, Beelzebub's hand snatching my arm is the only thing stopping me from dropping on my knees from its force. A war drum beats at the center of my chest, the darkness around us illuminating in a reddish hue. The feeling swirls like a tornado, nausea bringing bile to my throat. I've only felt this at times around the Holy ass Michael when he held me hostage, and when Lucifer had me up in the air the day Eric got hurt. *You also felt it few other times.* The thought fleets through my mind, but I can't concentrate enough to think about it.

"Helena?" The urgency in Beelzebub's voice helps me push the storm inside me away, at least enough to look up at him.

"A jinn." My lips are numb and barely moving enough to utter the word.

"Colt." Beelzebub's eyes widen, and I can tell he is torn between staying with me and leaving to make sure Colt doesn't end up like a shish kebab.

"Go!" Pushing his hands away, I clench my fists and stay standing on sheer will alone. "Go help him, I'll be right behind you." When he doesn't move, I snap at him. "Go fucking kill that piece of shit. I'm fine!"

After a long look, he sighs and bolts out on the street, heading straight at our enemies. Reaching a hand, I lean on the wall, the skin on my sweaty palm scraping over the bricks. *You can do this, Hel,* I tell myself sternly. *You can push away the crippling feeling and go nail the sucker. You are a hunter, damn it!* No one can say that being stubborn is always a bad thing. It keeps me standing and somewhat clear-headed. Another thought comes out of nowhere that snaps me out of the misery. *You are Satan's daughter. They should be afraid of you.* I still hate it. I hate knowing that fact, and I'll despise Lucifer forever for telling me that part of my parentage. But I can't ignore the fact that it helps me collect myself enough to not curl up in a ball and sob.

You are also the daughter of Zedkiel. Go send them back to rot in Hell.

A smile tilts my lips at that. I have my mother's blood in my veins, too, not just my father's. It's time the jinn learned not to fuck with this abomination.

Chapter Three

HELENA

A demon goes air born, his large body sailing through the air, heading straight in my direction. His gleaming, twisted horns turn right at me as I get closer, running at full speed toward the fight. Turning in a full circle without stopping my progress, I slice my dagger across his body from neck to crotch as he flies by me. The roar of pain is louder than the shouts and growls coming from the mass of bodies ahead of me. Black blood sprays in the air, splattering on the street in my wake.

I don't stop.

The demon might not be dead, but I know he is out for the count and won't be joining his buddies anytime soon. I felt the skin of my knuckles grazing his hide, which means my dagger cut deep. Deep enough to have his intestines spill out around him. Let him play with that for a while.

Colt roars, in anger or pain, I'm not sure which. I see his snarling face through the moving bodies of the three demons that have cornered him. Beelzebub is exchanging punches and kicks with the most enormous beast of the bunch, the cracking of bones and sound of flesh hitting flesh echoing like applause around us. Leaving the massive fallen angel to handle his foe, I whir off, heading straight for Colt.

The feeling that there is something powerful lurking around us doesn't go away, even when there is no one I can see to fit that description. My own power surges through me from my toes all the way to the crown of my head, raising goosebumps all over my skin. With clenched teeth, I push off the ground mid-sprint, and lifting the dagger high, I sail through the air, the red and golden runes on the blade sparkling like a ray of sunshine through stormy clouds, latching onto the back of the closest demon.

The monster is as giant as a truck, his back so wide I have to snake my free arm around his neck so I don't fall on my ass. With all the strength I can muster, I swing my dagger down, embedding it just below his ear so deep that my fingers sink inside his skin along with the top of the hilt. His horned head rears back, his face lifting to the skies as an inhuman sound belts from his chest, one that shatters all the remaining windows of the building the demons left behind when they started destroying my city.

His sudden movement forces me to flop around on his back, only my arm and the dagger keeping me anchored to him. The demon starts twisting, his survival instinct making him wilder. Blood pours from his neck, coating my fingers, and I almost lose my grip on my weapon. I see his clawed hand reaching out in an attempt to pull my blade away from his neck, the sharp points striking like shark teeth at my skin. With no other option, unless I'm willing to bleed and get us all killed, I release my dagger, my fingers wrapping around one of his horns.

The demon freezes and his whole body stiffens, stopping

the bull ride he iss giving me with his flailing. It's such an unexpected reaction, it stops me as well, making me consider the implications. Luckily, Beelzebub's roar snaps me out of it and, planting both my feet on the small of the demon's back, I release his horn and grab the hilt of the dagger again, yanking on it for all I'm worth.

Warm fluid splashes over my face a moment before the world starts tilting, and I feel gravity pulling me down. Blinking fast to clear my sight, I brace for impact, but an arm snatches me around the waist and deposits me on my feet in a whirl of movement. The body of the almost-decapitated demon falls on the ground with a heavy thump.

"You okay, she devil?" Colt gives me a quick glance over his shoulder.

He managed to reach me before the demon took me down with him, placing us back to back facing the remaining two monsters. They bare their large, sharp teeth at us, saliva dripping from them like they're rabid dogs.

"Peachy." Spitting out the blood that drips on my tongue when I speak, I wipe my face with a forearm.

"I can feel something powerful is here; I just can't see it." Sweeping my gaze around, I'm only met with empty streets. "It's here, though."

"Can you tell which direction?" Colt grunts when he kicks the attacking demon in his chest, sending him flying backward.

Almost bending in half, I avoid the reaching claws of the other demon that were aimed at my face, slicing his forearm open when he pulls back. "No." Panting, I push my back closer to Colt. "I only know it's close. Like, really close."

"We need to cut them down and go," Colt shouts to Beelzebub.

I know he spoke to the Archdemon because he got an answering sound, something between an affirmation and a growl. Apparently that is enough because both of them attack their opponents with renewed vigor. I follow suit.

The demon is still cradling his cut forearm when I throw myself at him. He obviously didn't expect it because his face looks comical when we collide. The force when my body hits his only makes him stagger but that's all I need. Ramming my knee in his groin, I double him over before shoving the dagger under his chin as deep as it'll go. His eyes roll to the back of his head, and he tips sideways, taking me down with him.

Jumping off the pavement, I plant my boot on his face and yank my blade out. Wiping it off his skin, I straighten up to find Beelzebub and Colt watching me with unreadable faces.

"What?" Searching around in case another of these creatures is ready to jump us, my shoulders relax when I don't see anyone around.

"We can talk when we are away from the open." Beelzebub leaves Colt with his mouth partially open, cutting off whatever he is about to say.

"Yeah, good idea." Walking between them, I head in the direction of the Sanctuary. "I can still feel the jinn, I think it's only watching us for now." Keeping my voice low, I'm hoping the thing can't hear us.

"We should lose it first," Colt mumbles from behind my left shoulder.

"No shit, Captain Obvious." Beelzebub snorts at my drawl. "I almost asked it if it wanted to come for a visit with us."

"I can't wait for my brother to wake up and deal with

you," Colt says incredulously. "I never thought I'd want to see his face as much as I do now."

"Huh. Being put in your place is a bitch, isn't it?" Smirking at him, I hide the smile that wants to lift my lips. "Let's take the jinn for a spin around the city, and you can tell us all about it."

Not waiting for his reply, I bolt down the street like an arrow, Colt's loud profanities and Beelzebub's laughter like a clap of thunder echoing behind me.

Chapter Four

HELENA

No matter how many loops we do around the city, getting to the point of double backing, going in circles, and whatnot, the damn thing is still following us and won't show itself. My legs are burning, and I develop a stitch in my side, but I can't stop moving. I have a feeling that if we stand in one place long enough to rest, it'll attack. Good thing we left Narsi to keep an eye on Eric until we get back. The stupid creature is even more deranged after coming through the portal, clinging to me like his life depends on it. I'm not sure the Trowe would've waited for the jinn to attack. If what I feel is, in fact, a jinn. As stupid as the creature is, he would've chased it down.

I stop in my tracks, and Colt bumps into my back.

"What's wrong?" Both Beelzebub and him push me between their bodies while searching the darkness for danger.

"Why are we running from it?" They turn slowly to look at me. Thinking about my sidekick gives me an idea. A stupid one, but a plan nonetheless. "It wants something, that's why it's following us and not gunning for our heads. We should force it to either attack or show itself."

"That is a terrible idea." Colt looks down his nose at me. "We can't take on a jinn, just the two of us." I raise an eyebrow at him. "You are not fighting a jinn." His hand slices the air.

Beelzebub groans, as if pained.

It looks like the enormous fallen is the smartest of them all since he figures me out. The shaking of his head, his mouth pressed in a white line on his handsome face, confirms it. Colt, on the other hand, squints at me, his jaw set as if that will scare me enough and I'll listen to his word vomit.

"Go on then, shoo!" Waving Colt off like the pesky fly that he is, I turn to Beelzebub. "How do you want to do this?"

The fallen looks like he wants to argue his point, despite knowing how useless it is, so I wait him out. I mean, I have a feeling the jinn will attack if we stand in one spot. So, I'll let them talk themselves to death if they want. It's a win-win situation for me, either way.

"I would've felt better if Leviathan was with us, as well." When my eyes narrow at him, he sighs. "I'm not worried we might get hurt, even if it's a disastrous idea to have you bleed. I'm more worried about them taking you, and the two of us not being able to stop it from happening."

Knowing he is right deflates my attitude, making me swallow everything I am about to spit at him. The white walls keeping me caged in the room Michael kept me in, while my eyes burned from the glare, comes to the front of my mind. It's difficult to suck in air, my lungs contracting with the panic of being imprisoned again. Realizing that I'm subconsciously scratching the arm in the exact spot they poked me and left bruises, I pull away the sharp nails and let my arm drop limply to my side.

"It's only one." I'm not even sure why I think I should point that out.

"We can't be sure." Beelzebub, seeing that I cracked under his logic, inches closer, his tall and broad frame blocking my view of Colt.

"But I am sure." Closing my eyes, I stop struggling with the feeling swirling in my chest. It has never been this strong before, and I don't want to think about what that means. "It's just one, I'm one hundred percent sure. No other demons are around either."

Beelzebub tilts his head, considering me. The open intrigue in his red eyes makes me want to shrink back and hide, but I clench my jaw. It's a little late for hiding now. Heaven and Hell know about the abomination that is Helena, no matter how much I want to wish it otherwise. I might as well own the freak that I am.

"Okay." The massive fallen rolls his shoulders.

"You cannot be serious!" Colt bursts from behind him. "This is fucking insane, even for you Beelzebub."

"Why is he still here?" My words are as dry as sandpaper.

"She will go regardless of what we say, Colt." Beelzebub turns his red glare at Colt. "I would rather be there to help her than allow anyone to take her and bring about the apocalypse."

The mention of the apocalypse is like a jolt through my system. Me being hunted and on the top of the kill list for Heaven or Hell is one thing. After this long, I kind of got used to that idea. Me bringing the apocalypse on us all is on a whole new level of fucked up. Body numbed from the shock that particular word causes, I can only blink at the two men standing around me.

"Oh, nice." Colt sneers. "You thought this started because of you, and it would end with you if you fuck up, huh? And you call me self-centered?"

The air around us stirs, and every breath I take burns through my throat and lungs, brimming with power. Whatever rebuttal I had for the asshole gets lost in the thundering of my heart and the answering rage that feeds the anger in my chest. My new power pulses like a ticking bomb inside me, giddy to be unleashed on whoever is trying to hurt me. The ground under our feet shakes violently, causing cracks to spread through the concrete like spider veins.

"Breathe, Helena," Beelzebub says calmly, learning the trick from Eric. "Deep breaths, sweetheart, we don't want to hurt everyone around us, do we?"

My old self rears her head when he calls me sweetheart. I want to shove my boot up his ass for giving me another stupid nickname. What the fuck is it with men and their crazy idea that we like being called pet names anyway? What? Our names are not good enough for them or something? Regardless of all that, his words help me control my untamed power, so I drop it. I can deal with him later.

Unwilling to stay in the open any longer like a sitting duck, I look around for a good place to have this meet and greet with the jinn. Above the roughed-up buildings, Turner Field, the Braves stadium, sticks out invitingly. It's a perfect place to deal with this without getting any bystanders hurt. Not that there are any bystanders around. Apart from roaming demons, I haven't seen any humans since I got back from Hell.

Without a word, I turn around and bolt through the alleys

between shops on the far side of the street. There is no need to turn around and look if the two men are following. I can hear the pounding beat of their boots on the pavement. Darting left and right, climbing over wired fences and low walls, I get closer to Turner Field. A couple of times, one of them pushes me up when I scramble around, losing my grip or my footing in my haste to reach the stadium before we get intercepted. I might be some powerful abomination that everyone wants to get their hands on, but Spiderman I am not.

I don't thank them for the help. Neither one of them deserves gratitude for letting things get as messed up as much as they are. They'd been too busy with whatever shit they had going on in their realm. I used to blame myself for everything that happens around me. Not anymore. I never asked for this shit, and I'll be damned before I take responsibility for Heaven or Hell alike. While my thighs are burning from exhaustion, the potent air burning my lungs, and I'm running like my life depends on it, I make a firm decision. I'll hold them responsible for it. All of them.

And they will pay.

Reaching the wide area before Turner Field, I sprint with my last burst of strength across it, bypassing the giant ball standing in front of it, jumping over the metal bar of the gate where tickets are presented. If I was coming to watch a baseball game, that is. I'm here for a different kind of game right now, so I'm sure they won't mind. The tall glass walls at the bottom of the large building loom closer, and I see the reflection of all three of us, determination and anger set on all our faces. Colt and Beelzebub are right on my heels when I jump and kick the door open, shattering the glass. The tinkling sound as the pieces fall like rain around us is the only sound mingling with my harsh breathing.

Blinking to adjust my eyes when we enter the belly of the building, I don't slow down as I fly past the bars and fast food shops on my left. The doors leading to the seats gap like open mouths of hungry beasts on my right. Prickling power crawls on my skin, announcing the jinn being near. Forcing my heart to slow down, I suck in a harsh breath.

"We need to split up." Not turning around, my boots keep pounding the ground. "Just pick a door and go for it." Swinging my arm to point at the doors on my right, I keep running.

One set of thundering footsteps fades away. After a while, a second set disappears behind me, leaving only the sound of my running feet and the staccato of my heart accompanying me. Picking a random door, I go through it, and as soon as I reach the rows of plastic seats, I climb the stairs up towards the top as fast as I can. Lifting my face to see where I am, a groan escapes me when my gaze lands on the humongous billboard and the chopping cow next to it, whose arm cuts the air up and down every time the Braves score a homerun. What the fuck is it with these stupid billboards and cows everywhere I turn around? I can't think about what that may mean because I reach the top just as a burning power slams into my back. Diving for the first thing close by to hide from it, I tuck and roll, stopping in a crouch under something large that overshadows everything around me.

It's the stupid chopping cow.

Chapter Five

HELENA

Sliding my hand behind, gripping the hilt of the dagger, I pull it out. The comforting weight of the blade slows the panic bubbling in my stomach to a dull hum. Energy streams through my limbs, making my arms tingle and the runes on the dagger burst to life like a light show. Jerking my hand down to hide it from prying eyes, I curse under my breath. If the jinn didn't see where I hid, they now know because of my fireworks display.

"Chop, chop…" murmuring under my breath, I shake my head at my own stupidity.

Shadows twist and turn everywhere I look as I search for whoever hit me with the power. The blue plastic seats neatly lined in rows all around me are the only thing I see. Everything is dark, all the shiny glowing ads for companies sponsoring the baseball team blending in the night. The grass field at the center is only visible by the tiny glow of the new moon above my head. Straining my eyes, I try to see if I can spot Colt or Beelzebub anywhere. No such luck. I mean, obviously, since this structure was made to fit close to fifty thousand people comfortably, it's like looking for a needle in a haystack.

A low, amused chuckle whispers in the air, raising goose-bumps all over my arms and legs. The short hairs on the back of my neck stand on end, my breath hitching in my throat. Darting my eyes left and right is as helpful as a knife in a gunfight.

They are not trying to kill you, they just want to capture you, I tell myself sternly to push away the fear crawling up my spine.

I'm all talk, acting tough as shit while I'm scared out of my mind. I'll be stupid not to be afraid. It's not like I want to die or be tortured so entities can play a power game through me. All my sass only helps me push through the crippling feeling, so I hold onto it with all I've got. With that in mind, I straighten up.

"It's just you and me, coward, so why don't you show your face?" The calm of my voice hides the fact that my hands are trembling, and my palms are sweaty.

"A brave thing, calling me a coward." The words are just a purr in the wind impeding my attempt to pinpoint the direction of whoever speaks.

"Yeah, well, it's not me hiding from view now is it?" My taunting chuckle ends up sounding a little constipated, but whatever.

"You think you can stand against me, little girl? When millennia old creatures cannot?" There is no anger or animosity coming from the jinn, just pure curiosity.

"You came after me, all of you." Spitting the words, I grind my teeth. "I didn't ask for this. I didn't start it, but I have no other choice but to finish it thanks to you."

A cracking of plastic sounds off around us, echoing like a shotgun in the silence. My heart skips a beat before jackhammering in my chest. Swinging my body in that direction, I look around wildly to spot any movement, any shadow or outline telling me where the jinn is.

"They are getting closer, but not here yet." The jinn sounds like he is gloating. To my horror, his words drift from somewhere behind me, and I flip in that direction fast.

"What do you want?" Maybe if I keep him talking, I'll figure out where he is. "I'm sure you didn't follow me so we can chat."

"You picked a side." The hiss is so angry that I take an involuntary step back, almost toppling over the stupid cow's feet. "You should not have chosen any of them!"

"What the fuck dude!" Anger like no other races through me at his accusation. "I picked a side?" My body is vibrating with rage, the entire building groaning and shuddering from it. Glass bursts somewhere, the faded sound from it hitting the floor lost in the buzzing in my ears. "I picked my own side, you dumb fuck. It's a crime now to not want to be killed or be used as a fucking pawn?"

"First you side with the Heavens, now you side with Hell. It tips the balance, little girl." The words sound stronger, angrier, and a hell of a lot closer than I'm comfortable with. "We cannot let that happen. You must die."

Power surges through the air, enveloping me in it like a bubble. My whole body seizes, all my muscles clenching like someone just shoved a high-watt wire in my chest. It's so painful that my mouth hangs open, but no sound comes out, although the screams in my head are so loud I think my eardrums will burst from it. The hilt of the dagger bites into my skin, my fingers involuntarily tightening around it before I start convulsing, and losing any remaining energy, I drop on the ground.

The strength of it keeps increasing while I flop around like a fish out of water. Colors sparkle behind my closed eyelids, the pain so unbearable I'm not sure how I'm still alive. My heart should've exploded by now. Or maybe I died, and this will be my eternity, dealing with pain until the end of time. Forcing my eyes open to tiny slits only makes me wish I kept them closed. The statue of the cow is the only thing I see, one arm lifted, ready to start chopping. I wish it can chop off my head to stop the pain.

"Helena." The sound of my name snags my gaze away from the damn cow.

"Co…" My teeth clench hard, cutting off my words, and I almost bite off my tongue.

Colt walks up to my flopping body, his gaze scanning me from head to toe like I'm some worm that got stuck in the sole of his shoe. What the fuck? Why is he strolling around like he is in a park instead of helping me? Tears stream down my cheeks, hot rivulets sliding over my chilled skin, disappearing in my hair. His face blurs every time a new flood fills my eyes. A further thought strikes me in my delirious mind. Was Eric's brother working with Mammon and the jinn all this time? Did I let our enemy walk willingly among us? I know he dislikes his brother, but surely he doesn't want him dead. And where the fuck is Beelzebub?

Fire starts building in my chest. The burning hits so suddenly, and it's so strong that it overrides the pain still holding me in its grasp. A scream, a terrified, horrible sound that I never thought I can possibly make, is ripped from my throat. My back bows off the ground, almost snapping me in half. Oh, God, please let me die. Colt walks around me, still watching me like I'm some exhibit in a zoo. His boots stop right above my head, and I look up at his face with all the anger and hatred I can master portrayed in my eyes.

And then I blink.

Beelzebub is looking down at me, and there is no sign of

Colt. Another blink and Michael is smirking at my misery. Lucifer, Amanda, George, Jared, Cass, Hector, Raphael, Maddison, Eric... the faces keep flicking from one to the next, some of them I've never seen before in my life. They keep changing so fast I have to close my eyes so I don't look at it anymore.

"Not a coward anymore, am I?" The fucker is snickering like the deranged asshole that he is. "I thought you were tougher than this. What a disappointment you turned out to be, little girl." He is clicking his tongue in disappointment.

"Kill me!" That's the only thing I summon enough energy to say.

"Ah, ah, ah...I have other plans for you." His shoes scrape the ground, telling me he moved to my right. "We might even have some fun before you become useful for once in your life."

All sorts of depraved thoughts flash through my head behind my closed eyelids. The jinn is making me see things. Bile rises in my throat, the acid burning as strong as the fire trying to eat me alive. The rage I usually manage to push down with deep breaths, and Eric's calm presence, erupts from me with such strength I'm expecting my ribs to split open. My body lifts in the air, floating in front of the jinn, and my eyes snap open. My gaze locks with his, although I'm looking at him upside down, and the shock and disbelief that widens his eyes would be comical if I wasn't wishing I was dead. All his faces disappear, leaving a stunningly beautiful creature gaping openmouthed at me.

I have no idea what I look like, but the horrified expression replacing the shock and twisting his face makes me smile. *Take that fucker,* I think to myself before a dark blur barrels between me and the jinn. It tackles the creature, and

I drop on the ground with a sickening crunch of breaking bones. Beelzebub roars, and I turn my head to the side just in time to see the jinn disappear in a puddle of ash and smoke from under the wild and pissed off fallen angel.

"Helena!" Colt drops to his knees next to me, hiding Beelzebub from my view.

"I hope the fucker is dead…"

I'm not sure I say it out loud, but that's enough for me because at this point I couldn't care less. The pain is gone, and I feel so empty like I'm a speck of dust in the wind. Closing my eyes, I know nothing more.

Chapter Six

HELENA

Home.

The smell of home pulls me back to wakefulness. I can't explain the scent exactly, but it relaxes my muscles, and it makes it easier to breathe. The feeling of safety comes along with it, and I stretch my arms and legs. Well, I try to stretch them. A sharp pain shoots up my side and my right arm, and a pained gasp is ripped from my throat.

Everything comes back to me, the fight with the demons, running through Atlanta and my brush with death in the confrontation with the jinn. My eyes snap open. Although I still feel the pain, my body coils up so I can defend myself. Only the destroyed penthouse meets my searching gaze. There is no one here but me. Flopping my hands down, the fingers of my left hand glide through something silky and soft.

Eric's handsome face, his eyes still closed in a healing sleep, is there when I turn my head to see what I accidentally touch. Gliding my fingers gently through the feathers of his wings, I let his presence calm down the swirl of fear inside me. No wonder I smelled home before I fully woke up. Beelzebub and Colt laid me down next to Eric. His presence always anchors me. Even when he pisses me off, I feel safe around him.

"I really need you to wake up, monster boy." A lump forms in my throat, and his face gets blurry when tears sting my eyes. "I have a bad feeling I won't survive this round without you."

Eric doesn't answer, but he never does. I have tried coaxing him to come around before unsuccessfully. But he breathes, and that's enough for me right now. I inch closer to him, careful not to get on top of his wing. That's when I notice the idiots have moved him to the edge of the makeshift mattress so they could place me next to him. With effort, I push myself up and, kneeling, try to think of how I can pull him to the middle of it without jostling his hurt wing.

"What are you doing up?" Beelzebub's deep voice scares the shit out of me, and an embarrassing squeak passes through my lips.

I glare at him over my shoulder.

"What does it look like I'm doing asshole?" If I had the energy to stand up, I would so kick his ass right now. "I can't believe you pushed Eric on the edge to put me next to him. He is hurt for fuck's sake!"

"And you were not?" One eyebrow climbs up his forehead, his red eyes staring daggers at me. "Get back down before you lose consciousness again."

"I'm fine!" Snapping at him, I waddle around Eric on my knees, still contemplating how to move him. "Eric, on the other hand, is not."

Beelzebub is next to me faster than I can finish the sentence. Dropping on his knees, his fingers wrap around my shoulder firmly, and he stops my movement. His grip is not painful, but it's firm enough that there is no other option but to stop unless I want to fight him and make him release me.

"Do you remember everything that happened last night?" He searches my face, but my thoughts halt at his question.

Snapping my head around, I look at the floor-to-ceiling windows of the apartment. It's pitch black outside. Beelzebub said last night, which makes me hope the fallen doesn't understand how time moves in the human realm. Otherwise, I've been sleeping for over twelve hours easy. If not longer.

"We confronted the jinn tonight, right?" It sounds more like a demand for him to agree with than a question.

"No," Beelzebub says slowly, not looking away from me. "That was last night. We brought you here, and you were replenishing ever since." His thick fingers flex on my shoulder, "You expended a lot of power fighting him off, Helena."

My face burns with embarrassment at his words. Fighting the jinn off, my ass. Fighting to stay alive is more like it. Or wishing I was dead. Clearing my throat, I take a deep breath.

"Thank you for showing up when you did." See? I can be an adult and thank people, even when said people are fallen, and from Hell...oh fuck! "I'm sure he was going to kill me if you were a few moments late."

There! That's out of the way. Let's move on.

"What?" Beelzebub snorts the word, an incredulous look replacing the concern on his face. "I wanted to kill Colt because he listened to you and we separated. I have no idea what that fuck did to you, but I came too late, Helena. You destroyed him before I had a chance to fight him off you."

"Say what now?" Dropping my ass on my curled-up legs, I'm debating if the jinn messed with Beelzebub's head. "I couldn't fight him. He was ripping me apart from the inside out. I was burning alive when you got to me. I saw you tackle him."

"Yes." A tired sigh passes his lips, and he drops on the floor as well. "But the jinn was gone, and his essence burnt out of him. Do you remember exactly what you did?" He looks reluctant to say more but continues regardless of that. "You were glowing...fuck! I haven't seen anything like it in my entire existence. The power pulsing out of you..." he trails off again, my gut clenching from the expression of awe on his face. "It felt familiar and foreign at the same time. I got there first; I could've helped sooner, but you held me back. I've never felt so powerless. So...useless." His shoulders slump.

"You must be wrong." There is no other explanation, he must be. "My anger surged, yes, but I did nothing of the sort. I think I only managed to fight off the hold he had on me for a split second. That's when he showed his real face."

"You saw the jinn?" The shouted words bring Colt racing in the living room.

Beelzebub snaps his head at Eric's brother, eyes bulging in his head. I almost reach out to catch them in case they fall out of his sockets. An uneasy feeling churns inside my stomach. Colt strides purposely towards us, crouching next to Beelzebub and frowning at me.

"What's wrong with her?" His frown turns on Beelzebub.

"Really asshole? No matter what happens, your first

thought has to be that there is something wrong with me?" Hissing at him, I just glare at both of them.

I would've crossed my arms over my chest for emphasis, but my right one still hurts, and I settle on displaying my anger with my gaze. It would've been hilarious, and yes, I would've been gloating for days to see Colt flinch away from me as if scared. But Beelzebub's words that I destroyed the jinn pop uninvited into my head, and I almost hurl whatever is left in my stomach where I'm sitting.

"She saw the jinn," Beelzebub says faintly, awe, incredulity, and fear evident in his deep voice.

Colt plops on his ass, widening his eyes, matching his buddy's expression.

"What's the big fucking deal?" Angry that they don't tell me what's so weird about that, I snap at them. "We all know I'm not human, so what if I saw the jinn? Will I grow a second head now?" A thought strikes me, and my left hand flies to my head. "Will I grow horns? You better answer no to that question really fast or I'll stab you both in your sleep."

"No," both of them say at the same time.

It's like a weight has been lifted off my chest, and I almost smile. Almost. But these two killjoys won't keep their mouths shut if their lives depend on it.

"No one sees the true form of a jinn." Beelzebub mumbles and Colt nods firmly backing him up.

"You two do." Pointing an accusing finger at each of them in turn, I narrow my eyes. "Lucifer and the Holy asses, as well as Mammon, do, too."

My chest contracts when the two jerks shake their heads vehemently. A shiver races up my spine when Colt opens his mouth.

"No." His head is still shaking, the hair flopping around his forehead. "No one sees the true form of the jinn."

Well, Fuck!

Chapter Seven

HELENA

"Are you sure, sure? Or are the two of you just guessing here?" I sound very hopeful. There must be an explanation for this.

"We know of them, yes. We can tell--Beelzebub moves his head left and right slowly—"somewhat when we come face to face with one of them. Only if we are actively searching for the signs. Otherwise..." he trails off.

"Maybe I was hallucinating from the pain and the fact I was burning alive from the inside." I almost pat myself on the back for coming up with a plausible answer.

"Maybe..." Beelzebub looks thoughtful at that, and I already feel better.

Turning to see Colt is a terrible idea. The asshole is watching me with narrowed eyes, and I can tell he doesn't believe a word I said. My hand itches to slap the squinting look off his face.

"Where is Narsi?" Changing the subject is for Colt's sake. It has nothing to do with the anxiety trying to dig a hole in my stomach.

Beelzebub looks over my shoulder, and I twist around to follow the direction. I wish I didn't. My heart breaks in a million pieces when I spot the curled-up lump in the corner of the spacious living room. The Trowe looks so miserable and sad, tears prickle my eyes. Hugging his bony knees, his tiny body is squeezed into a tight ball, and his face is half hidden behind his legs. The eyeless sockets are still creepy as anything, but the sadness radiates from him in waves.

"Why are you hiding there?" I didn't see him because usually he is a ball of energy, and I was expecting to wake up to him clinging to whatever limb of mine he can get.

"The mistress doesn't want Narsi." He hisses, or whimper-hisses, at me. It's so low I can barely hear him.

"What the hell is wrong with you?" Frowning disapprovingly at him, I turn more to see him better. "Just because I left you to look after Eric while I was gone doesn't mean I don't want you." I don't tell him that I'm still not sure how smart it is that I brought him here with me. "I didn't leave you behind, did I?"

"I am tasked to protect you, not Shadow." He gets louder, hissing for real this time. "Mistress almost died while I watched Lucifer's spawn sleep."

"Hey!" At my snap, he jolts back, hitting his head off the wall. I glare at him. "That spawn is my mate. You should be honored I trusted you with his life."

"I care nothing about Shadow." The Trowe lifts his pointy chin stubbornly.

Beelzebub chokes, and Colt snorts. I ignore the jerks.

"Then you don't care about me either." Turning away from him, I wrap my fingers around Eric's leg.

Thankfully, no one came while all of us were scattered all over Atlanta. I have no doubt after hearing the damn creature he would've sat there gloating if anyone tried to hurt Eric. It's quite an unsettling thought. Why on earth do I trust all these creatures? Have I lost my mind?

"I can see your mind churning from here," Beelzebub says gently, his deep voice soothing despite the fact he is one of the rulers of Hell. "I can tell you now that whatever it is that you are thinking, you are wrong."

"What? You are a mind reader now?" I don't even look at him, still watching the rise and fall of Eric's chest.

"I don't need to read minds to know that the damn Haltija made you doubt all of us." The hurt in his words is unmistakable, so I lift my gaze to see him through my lashes. "None of us here want to hurt you, or Eric."

"Right." An unladylike snort escapes me. Not that I'm a lady or anything, I just don't usually snort. Mostly I only swear at anything and everything.

Beelzebub glances at Colt pointedly. From the corner of my eye, I can see Eric's twin grinding his teeth, his jaw clenched tight. The silence stretches, and when I'm about to tell them to get out of my sight, Colt's shoulders slump, and he blows out a deep breath.

"I might dislike his snobby ass"—Colt glares at Eric, and I'm debating grabbing my dagger—"because he acts like he is better than the rest of us, and that makes me do everything I can to piss him off. But no...I don't want to see my brother dead."

Turning my face towards him, I squint at him, pursing my lips. He will need to do much better than that if I am to believe him. All I needed was one day to learn what kind of an ass Colt is. I know better than to go along with what he just said.

"I'm telling the truth." His cheeks pinken slightly as if having an honest conversation is outside his comfort zone. "Don't get me wrong, I don't mind if he gets hurt. The asshole deserves it for having a stick up his ass. But I will kill anyone who tries to see him dead."

He is a demon Hel, and telling the truth is outside of his comfort zone, my mind chirps, but I push the thought away. It's my old conditioning rearing its ugly head and making me distrust others based on species alone. All of them are twisting the truth to fit their needs. *And you are Satan's daughter if you want to get technical about it,* I remind myself.

Yeah, let's not forget that little pearl, shall we?

Leviathan storms inside the apartment like a whirlwind, and all three of us jump to our feet. This time, when Narsi latches to my leg, I don't freak out, and I don't use him like a football. I guess he forgets that he is upset with me for leaving him to keep watch over Eric. My fingers tangle in his messy locks, holding him in place in case he decides to throw himself at the dragon dude. Putting my weight on the balls of my feet, I tense, ready to attack whoever is coming on his heels.

"Stand down." Leviathan lifts his paw-sized hand, as if that means shit to me.

My mouth opens to tell him where to stick his bossy attitude, but it stays hanging open when Raphael walks through the front door. The Archangel looks like he was fighting a pack of feral wolves. His always-impeccable clothing hangs in tethers on his large body, the skin under the rags cut and bleeding in so many places that it looks red instead of the usual alabaster.

He stumbles inside, his breaths short and his yellow eyes wild when he looks around. As soon as his gaze locks on mine, I can't stand frozen in place anymore. Pushing the Trowe away, I bolt for him. Raphael opens his arms, and I wrap mine around him just in time to stop him from collapsing on the floor.

"Why are you just standing there." Snapping at the idiots gaping at Raphael, I almost fall down with him when his entire weight falls on me. "Help me, you jerks."

Beelzebub is next to me in a second, followed by Colt. They each grab an arm, hiking the Archangel over their shoulders. Raphael's eyes are still wild and unfocused, but they clear out when he hears my voice.

"Helena," Raphael rasps, and I want to scream and kill whoever did this to him. "You are safe." With that last murmur, his eyes roll to the back of his head and his face dropping toward his chest.

"What did you do to him?" Whirling on Leviathan, I'm ready to take all my anger out on him.

"I did nothing!" Looking down his nose at me, he speaks through his teeth. "He opened the portal to Heaven right in front of me and dropped at my feet. It's them that did this to him."

Jerk or not, Leviathan grabs me before I hit the floor when my knees give out from under me.

Chapter Eight

HELENA

Luckily, I don't stay unconscious for long, unlike other times when I wake up after a day, or a few days if going nuclear in Hell counts. I blink my eyes open, trying to focus on my surroundings, while Leviathan is still doing his best to lay me down gently next to Eric. The fact that they haven't yet moved my mate to the center of the makeshift mattress is not lost on me. Seeing Raphael bloodied and pale on the dirty floor to my right pushes that annoyance to the back of my mind.

"Put Raphael next to Eric." Swatting Leviathan's hands away from me, I roll over on my knees. "There is nothing wrong with me. Him, on the other hand...he looks like he is about to die." My stomach lurches with that thought.

"He will be well; he just needs to recover." Dragon boy sounds bored while he scowls at me.

Ignoring his arrogant ass, I wave my hand at Beelzebub and Colt to indicate they shouldn't stand around like lumps but do what I asked. Obviously bringing them here came with a side effect for them and a perk for me. I get to boss them around like they're my personal assistants instead of fallen angels and, in Colt's case, one of their spawns. Oh, well. They're more than welcome to go back to Hell for all I care. My main concerns at the moment are Eric and Raphael. What on earth happened to the Archangel while he was in Heaven? And does it have anything to do with the fact that he helped me escape the Holy ass, Michael?

Beelzebub moves to do my bidding without comment as if listening to me is the most natural thing in the world. I think I like him more than the rest of them so far. Colt is a different story. His face twists in a grimace that scrunches up his nose, like he smelled something foul, when he reluctantly follows the other fallen. They lift the Archangel, none too gently to my dismay, dragging him next to Eric.

"You'll hurt him more." Scurrying up, I help them as well by grabbing one of Raphael's legs. "You don't have to like him, but if any of you so much as hurt a hair on his head, there will be hell to pay."

"You think you have a say in it, little girl?" Leviathan growls from behind me, setting my teeth on edge.

"Dude, feel free to get your ass back where you came from." Squaring off my shoulders, I swallow the anxiety threatening to choke me with his presence alone. "I came to Hell so I can close the gate, not because I'm picking sides. From where I'm standing, all of you want to either use me or kill me. You'll excuse me if I pick my own side."

The silence that follows my words is deafening. All the air in the room gets charged with anticipation, crackling with the power that emanates from the three conscious men with me. Raphael releases a barely audible groan, but there is no peep from Eric. I almost jump out of my own skin when Narsi hisses angrily and crawls on all fours to stand between Leviathan and me.

"You will do good not to threaten my mistress, Leviathan." The creepy sound of the Trowe's voice raises goosebumps on my arms. "Satanael might be missing, but he surely is not dead. He will skin you alive if a hair is missing from her head by your hand."

"I can't say I disagree with the Haltija, brother." Beelzebub straightens to his full height. "The girl is not to be harmed."

"The girl is right here!" Spitting the words at them, I clench my fists.

I hate that the fire is missing in my voice, but what Narsi said is messing with my head. I don't want them destroying my world or hurting angels and Archangels alike. That still doesn't mean I'm all happy about being protected by Satan, regardless if he is my father or not. Uneasiness drills holes in my stomach.

"Will you please tell us what happened to Raphael?" In hopes to defuse the situation, I let the argument drop. "Where exactly did you find him?"

Leviathan glares at Beelzebub and Narsi for a long time before his icy-blue gaze settles on me. Everything inside me stills, almost as if even my soul wants to hide and stay unnoticed by his penetrating eyes. My dagger warms up, and I can feel it's power pulsing at my lower back. I hate being grateful to Beelzebub and Colt for making sure my weapon is where it belongs, but I am. Not moving a muscle, I let the fallen stare at me as long as he likes. At least my GPS is not going crazy at his nearness, so there is that.

"I was looking for any information that can give us an advantage." Leviathan grumbles, his words pushed through his teeth as if it's hard for him to have to explain himself. "I was at the destroyed place you told us Lilith's daughter had her office." I guess he is still refusing to acknowledge

Maddison by name. I don't correct him because it's point-less. "I found nothing there, not even a trace of the wards. As I was leaving, the gate opened and he dropped at my feet."

"Okay..." I wait him out because I can tell there is more to it.

"I tried to go through the portal." Leviathan lifts his chin, cranking up the chilly look in his eyes, daring me to say a word about his confession. "The one you are protect-ing." He stabs an accusing finger at Raphael's sleeping form. "And the one that even half dead, he fought to stop me from going through."

"Good for him." When he snarls at my words, I glare at him. "What? Your place is not there, and there is no reason for you to cross that portal. We have enough problems without that."

"I do not wish to destroy Heaven, girl!" Leviathan grinds his teeth, "I needed to find Michael. It's him that started all of this. Him, or your mother." He spits the word mother like it's a bug that went in his mouth by accident.

"It's jinn that started all of this, so you can stop blaming Michael or my mother." Like hell I'm going to let him point the finger at the angels so the fallen can have their butts clean. "Isn't that what Lucifer said? Or all of that was bull-shit so you guys could manipulate me? You won't be the first, I'll tell you that much."

Beelzebub sucks in a breath, making his massive chest puff up, and I know what he is planning on saying. For some reason, I really don't want Leviathan to know that I saw the pure form of the jinn. Petty? Maybe, but I only have my instincts to rely on right now.

"Can we try to help both of them wake up?" I face Beelzebub, turning my back on the pissed off dragon. "We need to know what happened to Raphael. And he may know what happened to the rest of my friends."

To my surprise, it's Colt that comes to my rescue. "There is nothing more we can do for my brother. He will wake up when he wakes up." Walking around the makeshift mattress, he runs a hand over Eric's body as if testing his theory. "I'm not sure why he is not healing." His green eyes snap to my face, and my heart gives a hard, painful thud. They are so much like Eric's. "For the Archangel, however, I think we can help. I'm just not sure he will appreciate it when he wakes up." Colt gives me a smirk.

Swallowing thickly, I look from Colt to Beelzebub. The huge fallen has his lips pressed firmly, obviously unhappy that we stopped him from spilling the beans. His red eyes are narrowed, and his plate-sized hands are fisted at his sides. My blood rushes through my veins and buzzes in my ears. I don't look away from Beelzebub, letting him make up his mind.

"He can handle himself." Nostrils flaring, Beelzebub turns away from me. "If anyone can deal with this, it'll be Raphael." He crouches opposite Colt, placing Eric and Raphael between them. "Make sure she doesn't interfere."

The last words confuse me, and I frown at the back of his head. Make sure *who* doesn't do *what* now? I have no time to wonder or even ask him what he meant. Leviathan wraps himself around me like a giant anaconda, immobilizing me a second before Raphael roars. Beelzebub and Colt hold their hands above him from opposite sides, and an orange glow pours from them into the Archangel's body. I swear my heart jumps all the way up to the back of my throat when I realize what they're doing. They are feeding his body with powers from Hell.

"No!" My scream is so high pitched that my ears start ringing. "Stop! You'll kill him! No!"

My arms and legs are held by Leviathan, preventing me from doing anything but scream. I try full body jerks in hopes to dislodge him, but he just tightens his hold. He is squeezing me so hard I can barely suck in air to breathe, but I don't give up. While he is too busy making sure none of my limbs can move, I bend forward and swing my head back with all the strength I can muster. The sickening crunch of his nose is very satisfying. Leviathan flings me away from him, his shout bouncing off the walls. Landing in a heap on the ground, I flop around before throwing myself at Beelzebub. We roll on the dirty floor for a few feet, stopping with him sprawled on his back and me straddling his chest. My dagger is already pressed right above his Adam's apple. His eyes widen, and he doesn't try to push me off him. He is not even trying to speak to defend himself. The only sound is Leviathan still cursing in what I believe is a demonic language, but it's guttural and strange to my ears.

"Helena?" Raphael's voice stops me from slitting Beelzebub's throat. "Don't, Helena." Coughing weakly, Raphael sighs. "They healed me."

Chapter Nine

HELENA

I'm still staring at Beelzebub's red eyes. He is watching me calmly, and I don't even think he is breathing. Hearing what Raphael said makes me feel horrible, and I roll off him, embarrassed. The fallen has been kind to me from the start. He didn't deserve my dagger against his throat. Not knowing what to say, while he is still stretched out on the floor not moving an inch, I walk to the Archangel. I'm not ready to apologize yet.

"Raphael." I breathe his name in relief, then squat next to him. "What happened? Who did this to you?"

"Jinn..." The Archangel props himself up on one fore-arm, his yellow eyes hollow without their usual spark. "Everything...everyone..." Shaking his head, he takes a deep breath, releasing it slowly. "It's chaos."

Leviathan and Beelzebub are around me in a second when my gaze connects with Colt, who is still kneeling next to Eric. I'm finding it difficult to breathe until Narsi shoves his little body under my arm, his tiny hands fisting my pants. As messed up as it may be, his nearness calms my panic. The Trowe might be creepy as hell, but I know he neither plans to kill me nor to manipulate me.

"They infested Heaven as well?" Beelzebub growls, his deep voice like bass vibrating through me.

Raphael scrubs a hand over his face. "Michael is missing…"

"Yeah, I kinda figured that after Lucifer explained about the jinn." Unable to keep my hands to myself, I reach for Raphael's, squeezing it reassuringly. "It explains why he was acting like a psychopath and keeping me prisoner."

"I don't know what to think anymore." Raphael's hand tightens on mine, and I can feel my bones grinding. "This will bring the end of the worlds if it keeps going. It's spilling out in all the realm. Angels are dying, lashing out at everything and everyone. They don't know who to trust. I nearly lost my life facing off with Gabriel. He was acting crazed, not believing it was really me. I didn't want to fight him, but it didn't convince him of the truth. I had to open the gate to save myself, and that's when Leviathan found me. I remember thinking and hoping Helena was safe when I fell through the portal, so I think it spat me out close to you because of that. Leviathan did bring me here after all."

"It's the same in Hell. We need to put an end to this." Leviathan starts pacing, the thumps of his heavy boots on the floor echoing around us. "It has gone out of control. We are chasing our tails here. What we need to do is find Mammon and kill the fucker. He started it, and it'll end with him."

Beelzebub and Colt launch into a heated discussion, giving Leviathan ideas on how they can execute his crazy idea, ignoring everything the Archangel said. Their voices keep rising, all three of them shouting as if whoever is loudest has the best plan. The noise falls to the background the longer I keep my gaze locked with Raphael's. The Archangel is ignoring the fallen as well, watching me curiously. He is still covered in his own blood, but at least he is not pale anymore, and all the open wounds have healed.

Out of everyone, Eric and Raphael are the only two people that have proven with actions that they care about me and don't want me hurt. No manipulation, no agendas. They have protected me and put their own lives in danger to do so. I know I can count on them. Only if Eric was awake, too. But he is not, and I only trust Raphael in this group of mismatched allies.

"We need to pick off the jinn and send them back to wherever they came from." I know Raphael hears me even through the shouts. His eyes widen. "It's the only way, Raphael. I don't think anyone controls them, not anymore."

"Why do you say that?" He swings his legs to the side to face me, lifting his knees up. "I mean you no harm, Helena. I only want to help."

"I'm not even sure it's about me anymore. Not only me, I should say." I notice the shouting stopped, and I can feel three intense stares on me, but I stay focused on Raphael. "We had an encounter with a jinn." Waving my hand, I point vaguely at Beelzebub, Colt, and me. "He said they want Heaven and Hell and have no problem destroying my body and soul to achieve that."

A tremor passes through me, and I shiver, remembering the deprived thoughts the jinn projected in my head. Cold sweat washes over me, beading on my forehead and upper lip. For all my bravado and sass, I can admit only to myself that I've never been this terrified in my life. Not even standing in front of Lucifer himself in the depths of Hell, or facing a pissed off Michael with his lightning ready to strike me, scared me this much.

Raphael is always relaxed, smiling, or wary. I've only seen him in those three states, plus the occasional annoyance when Eric was a jerk. But he reads my reaction without me saying a word. My body jolts back when his features darken, his yellow, warm eyes flashing dangerously and glowing with a golden light. Him being so nice and kind made me forget that the Archangel is a warrior as well. A muscle jumps in his jaw, and the energy coming off him seers my skin like I'm being slowly roasted. It reminds me that not long ago, the jinn was burning me alive from the inside out. I can't stop my panic at that thought. Anger at feeling helpless surges through me, rocking the building so strongly the three fallen topple over, rolling on the floor. Raphael is not moving, his own anger clashing with mine and feeding it more. The windows rattle, and the walls shudder, but there is nothing I can do to stop it. Narsi clings to me, whimpering softly.

"Raphael, stop! She'll bring the building on our heads!" Colt shouts from somewhere.

"You need to stop, Raphael! We will live, she may not!" Beelzebub roars.

Raphael's face clears out so fast my own anger is sucked out of me along with it, sending me tilting to the side. The Archangel grabs my arms to keep me from hitting my head on the unforgiving floor. Narsi hisses like a deranged cat, scratching at his arms, and Raphael yanks them back, glaring at the Trowe. I guess my sidekick has boundaries on what he will allow before he goes feral.

"I'm sorry, I didn't mean…" Raphael looks pained. "I'm sorry." Deflating, his shoulders slump, his head hanging down on his chest.

"What the fuck was that?" Leviathan is not the one to mix words.

"Raphael's empathy picked up on Helena's fear, and he acted on impulse," Beelzebub explains nonchalantly, like some twilight therapist to Archangels and abominations.

I gape at him.

"I have a domain in Hell, yes. I also have a brain despite that." Throwing his head back, Beelzebub laughs in my face.

Now that it's easier to breathe, and there is no one throwing testosterone in the air like one of those air fresheners that will spray you in the eyes if you walk past them, a million questions push to the front of my mind. One is the most important to me.

"Where are Hector, Maddison, and my team?" I hold my breath, waiting on Raphael to answer.

"Hiding in the ruins of the building where Michael held you, prisoner." His mouth twists unhappily. "It was the only place we thought no one would look for us."

"What are we waiting for?" Jumping up, I'm ready to bolt out of the room. "Let's go find them and bring them here."

Narsi tightens his hold on me, hanging like a koala from fear that I'll leave him behind. Looking at Eric's face, I feel torn on what to do. It's not like we can drag him around the city with us. But I don't want to leave him here without anyone watching his back.

"I'll stay." My eyebrows hit my hairline when Colt plops down next to Eric. "Just don't be too long or I might use him as a punching bag."

"You wouldn't dare!" I take a step towards him, but Beelzebub grabs my arm.

"Stop frustrating her, whelp, or I'll put you in your place." Beelzebub glares at Eric's twin.

I'm sure I would've gotten involved more if I wasn't

staring at the Archangel. Raphael is turned with his back to me, facing Eric. His hands are flat above my mate's chest, fingers splayed, the green glow emanating from them and entering Eric's body. My heart jackhammers painfully. Prayers jumble in my head that this will help. That Eric will wake up. The glow fades, and I gasp.

The hole from the claw on Eric's chest is closed. Only smooth skin glides under my fingers when I drop on my knees next to the Archangel. Cupping Eric's face, I wait unblinking for him to open his eyes. When long moments pass and nothing happens, a tear trickles down my face before I can stop it.

It didn't work.

Ignoring the four men plus the Trowe staring at me, not wanting to see the pity in their eyes, I scrub my face with a forearm. I'll find another way to wake him up, even if I have to capture a jinn and bleed him dry on top of Eric.

"I will try again when we come back." Raphael squeezes my shoulder, and I have to swallow the sob that's fighting to be set free.

"Yeah, we can try later. Let's go find the rest before it's too late." Avoiding their gazes, I grab the Trowe by the hand and walk out the front door.

Chapter Ten

HELENA

We follow Raphael through the city. The Archangel may look like he went through the wringer, but whatever Beelzebub and Colt did healed him completely. He keeps looking over his shoulder, making sure I'm still there. Not like I can run away, even if I wanted to. The two fallen are guarding my back, one on each side. Narsi crawl-walks on all fours, his head twisting around while he looks for threats.

The anxiety is still like acid in my stomach. At this rate, if there will be no place left for me on any realm that won't remind me of the time I almost died. Seriously. I can really use a break. My hopes that the damn building will look similar to Maddison's office see a sudden death when we finally reach the street.

Raphael stops, gliding over a yellowed lawn to a half-demolished two-story home. We all follow his lead, my fingers wrapping around the dagger as we blend in with the darkness. The weight of the weapon in my palm soothes my anxiety somewhat.

"It doesn't look like anyone is around waiting, but we

53

can't be sure," Raphael whispers without turning to look at us.

He is leaning to the side of the half-broken wall, watching the street. Beelzebub and Leviathan slink in the shadows, and not even I can tell exactly where they are standing. At least Narsi is quiet, but I wouldn't put it past him to start hissing or whimpering for no apparent reason. As if he knows I'm thinking about him, craning his neck, his face lifts to look at me, a disturbing smile shimmering on it. Blowing a slow breath through my lips, I yank him closer to me.

"I will check from the air." Leviathan grunts right behind my ear, and a second later, he when I elbow him in the gut.

"I have a kneejerk reaction if you invade my personal bubble." As far as apologies go, mine is lacking big time. A grin pulls my lips up so high my cheeks hurt.

Beelzebub chuckles.

"If the three of you are done,"—Raphael frowns at me disapprovingly, and my face burns in embarrassment—"some help might be handy." Turning to watch the street again, he keeps murmuring. "It's too quiet, I don't like this."

"Everywhere we've been in Atlanta has been too quiet after I got back from Hell." I point out the obvious. "Demons running around destroying everything can have that affect." Raphael looks at me like I've lost my mind. "Unless you've been gone as long as Eric and I, I'm sure you've seen this before."

"It's too quiet," he repeats slowly. "There is no sound at all, apart from the five of us."

And that's when I genuinely notice it. On the way here I was too tense, expecting an attack at any moment, as well as lost in my own thoughts about unimportant things. I wasn't paying attention to the sounds unless they were too close for comfort. Right now, there is nothing but the breaths coming from us. No hoots and distant screams that have been constant since I got back. No sounds of buildings collapsing or glass breaking. Not even the sound of insects or birds. Almost like the street is holding its breath.

"I don't feel jinn." My lips don't move when I mumble the words softly.

A line forms between Raphael's eyebrows and he tilts his head. From the corner of my eye, I see Beelzebub shaking his head subtly when the Archangel's gaze flicks to him. I don't have to see Leviathan to feel his penetrating stare, but at least he doesn't say anything. I'll count it as a small victory.

"Do you feel anything else?" Beelzebub asks softly, although his deep voice carries. "Anyone else but us?"

I shake my head, not wanting to add to the noise we are making no matter how low. The silence is unnerving. Not like in Maddison's office, but close. I'll never forget that deafening silence that made me feel like I'd go insane. Goosebumps prickle my arms just thinking about it.

Narsi releases his hand from mine and I look down at him. The Trowe glances from me to the street and back a few times before pressing his mouth in a firm line. I have no time to realize what he is planning before he bolts like an arrow out of our hiding spot right at the building.

My breath gets stuck in my lungs.

"Stupid Haltija!" Leviathan hisses angrily, and for the first time, I agree with him.

My sidekick definitely has a few screws loose. He is not even trying to hide. Running on all fours faster than anyone I've seen, he reaches the ruined building in no time. The front of it looks somewhat intact, not counting the broken front door and busted windows. The back is entirely missing, like someone has taken a serrated knife and hacked the hell out of it. Narsi crawls up the front steps, reaching the gaping door before he turns around and lifts to his full height. He is tiny, but he looks intimidating, especially when he is baring his teeth like he is doing right now.

I'm about to go join him when he just stands there, but the three men with me surround me on all sides, pressing me too close between their massive bodies. I prickle at their attitude, hating the fact that they are stopping me from seeing what is going on. Taking a deep breath and preparing to elbow my way out of here, I almost choke when the air gets charged with power. It's not as strong as that of a jinn, but it's nothing to scoff at. It's also oddly familiar.

"What are you doing here, Haltija?" a familiar voice splits the quiet air on the street.

Clenching my fists so hard, I can feel my nails ripping the skin of my palms. The warmth of my blood only fuels my anger more. I can't put my finger on where I've heard the voice, but I need to calm down so I don't give us away, and so I don't make this entire street shake like an epicenter of a seven-degree earthquake. Concentrating on my breaths, I strain my ears to hear it again. Maybe it'll come to me. I don't miss that the three men around me stiffen when whoever it is speaks.

"I'm looking for Mammon," Narsi hisses, and my eyes almost pop out of my skull. What the hell?

"Is that so? And why would Mammon want to see you?" A husky chuckle numbs my brain. I know that voice. "Hell didn't teach you how to properly lie, I see. Who did you bring here, huh? Mammon will reward me greatly when I bring him your hide."

"I come alone!" Narsi's hiss turns eerie, but I'm not leaving him to deal with this alone.

Releasing the control on my anger, I unleash it like a whip. The ground rattles violently, the yards and street cracking open and splitting like veins. The three men around me stumble away, and I push my way out from between them. The ground is still shaking when I zero in on my target, striding down the street like I own it.

"Hello, Lauren." A menacing smile stretches my lips. "Long time no see."

Chapter Eleven

COLT

It's strange to walk in the human realm. I've always despised my brother for choosing it over Hell. For choosing humans over…me. I know that my father is the one that drove the wedge between my twin and me, comparing us in everything, pushing us against each other. Not like we stopped him, so both of us are to blame for that too.

Seeing Helena ready to stand up to anyone, including Lucifer himself, to protect my twin is like a sharp sword through my chest. Again, he gets the better bargain in life after being banished by my father and losing his wings. She gave him his wings back, as well. There is more to her than any of us know. It's as plain as anything that she is just coming into her powers, and she already faced a jinn and lived to tell the tale. Fallen and Archangels will be hard pressed to fight a jinn off or kill it. None are able to see their pure form.

"What in the name of the fates did you create, Satanael?" Musing loudly, I watch my brother sleep.

As painful as it is to admit, I'm glad it's Eric dealing

with the she-devil. I will never admit it, but I'm not sure I can handle her. And if I really want to be truthful to myself, I'll say that she even scares me. Helena is way too reckless, letting her emotions guide her actions more than her brain. I'm an arrogant bastard, I'll never deny it, but my self-preservation is at the top of my list. I turned my back on my twin out of logic and the selfish need to protect myself. I have no idea why I'm riling myself up and why these thoughts start swirling in my head, but there is nothing I can do to stop them.

The crazy female has no self-preservation instincts at all. She barges into any fight, no matter how futile it is to protect those she sees in need of it. Damn, she brought four of us from Hell to defend us from Mammon. A hunter trained by the Order from Heaven saving fallen. Regardless of her bloodline, she is something special, something different. Satanael wouldn't have done any of it, and neither would Zedkiel.

"What is she brother?" My eyebrows dip low over my eyes as I chew on my lower lip. "Do you even know what creature your mate is? From where I'm standing, soon she'll be able to slaughter us all if it strikes her fancy."

My heart rams against my ribs in a painful lurch. An uneasy thought pushes from the background in a warning that this is not normal behavior, but it disappears before I can grasp it properly. I realize I actually do believe that Helena can kill us on a whim. Maybe not right now, but in a not so distant future, I have no doubt there will be nothing and no one that can stop her if she decides to go on a killing spree. Is that why Michael wanted to get rid of her? Not wishing to advertise that even Heaven fears what she can become, he used her bloodline as an excuse to end her life?

"And you stopped him!" Growling angrily at Eric, I

grind my teeth. "You protected something that can destroy us all."

"I better be mistaken, and you are not talking about my mate, brother." Eric's eyes snap open, and I glare back at him.

"Is she your mate? Or her power blinded you to see what she wants you to see?"

"This is a new low, even for you." Disgust is evident in his voice, so I have no doubt he is not thinking clearly. Why can't he see the truth?

Pushing off the bundled rags under him, Eric sits up, rolling his shoulders. His wings lift up and down while he tests their weight, so I glare at them too. He shouldn't even have those back. Maybe the she-devil already has full control over him, turning him into something else as well. What if the jinn were sent to keep the balance by destroying these two? What if they are in the right? That last thought is like a slap in the face, and I jump up, crouching low next to my brother, shaking off whatever compulsion they were doing on me.

"Fuck!" Eric jolts back at my outburst, but I yank him down with me. "We have company."

He stiffens at my words, turning in a fluid motion to crouch next to me. Pointing at the far side that leads to the kitchen, he blends in with the shadows and is gone. I glide soundlessly on the opposite side, my entire focus on the door. I should've known something was wrong when all my thoughts got twisted and paranoid. Instead, like a fool, I was stewing in anger and almost attacked my brother.

The door cracks, but it doesn't fully open. I guess they know we are aware of them now. Creeping closer, I reach the wall next to the door and lift up, pressing my back to it. My claws lengthen, sharpening as I stretch my fingers. I missed out on fighting the jinn yesterday, but I'll make up for it now.

Eric materializes on the other side of the door, his horns already extended, his eyes burning with rage. I'm sure by now that he is aware that Helena is not here, and I can only imagine what kind of thoughts are going through his head. My mouth opens so I can tell him she is alive at least, but one of his claws lifts up, silencing me. His head tilts closer to the wall, and I follow his lead.

A tapping sound, like someone is trying to send a code through the wall, makes me frown. My gaze flicks to Eric, and I see the confusion on his face too. What in the worlds is going on? Before I have a chance to figure out who is playing games with us, the wall I'm leaning on explodes, sending me flying through the wall-to-ceiling windows, and I plummet to the ground.

Chapter Twelve

ERIC

I'm not sure how exactly I ended up back in this realm, and all I can think of at the moment is I need to find Helena. The last thing I remember is the crippling pain when a claw sunk in my chest. I had no time to even fear for her life or my own. It all went blank.

Now here I am, home.

Not just home, but with my twin brother next to me, mumbling angrily and cursing my mate. If I didn't need information so I can search for her, I will happily ended his miserable existence the moment I my eyes opened. I might not know anything else, but I still feel the warmth that was surrounding me in the void.

When the claw pierced my skin, sinking so close to my heart, I was sucked into a cold black hole, my soul shrinking from the iciness creeping inside me. It felt like it lasted forever, yet from one moment to the next, it was replaced by something warm. Something keeping the darkness that was trying to eat my soul away. It lulled me into the comfort that I feel ashamed of right now. I should've fought to find my way out. I should've struggled to shake off whatever it was so I could get back to Helena. To protect my mate.

Now, after being yanked by a glow from my warm cocoon not long ago, I'm back in my apartment with no one but my estranged brother next to me. Not what I expected, nor what I wanted, at any rate. I was ready to grab him by the neck and demand answers, but we got interrupted. First, I'll remove this threat, then I'll drill Colt for answers. Watching him pale across from me while we plaster ourselves on each side of the front door does not sit well with me. For someone wanting to be one step ahead of everyone, I sure as fuck don't feel all that great right now.

And what the fuck happened to my place?

Tilting my head, I hear the tapping on the wall, frowning at the sound. Is this some sick joke? What exactly are we dealing with here? The Order, the Archangels or Mammon? I have no time to even hype up my anger when a blast sends both of us flying across the vast living room. Colt hits the floor-to-ceiling windows first, bursting the glass into a shower of shards pelting our bodies before he goes down. I follow right behind him, the slicing of the broken window keeping me alert.

Colt is limp, which tells me the blast must've been closer to his side to render him unconscious. His body flips in the air, spiraling to the ground that's raising to meet us. I unfold my wings, righting myself in the air before arrowing in his direction. My wings are pressed close to my body to give me more speed, and I manage to scoop him up just before he hits the ground. I can feel the concrete graze my front for a second before I lift up again, soaring in the night.

Reaching enough altitude, I hover in the air with my twin draped over my arms, shocked at the sight before me. The city is in flames. Fires burn everywhere, the flames reaching for the dark sky like gruesome fingers. Skyscrapers and buildings stand like broken shards. Entire areas have been leveled to the ground, leaving empty patches sprinkled around the horrid distraction of Atlanta.

Colt jolts awake in my arms, and I look down at him. Anger boils in my veins from seeing my home destroyed. If any of them had anything to do with this, our petty scuffles would be child's play compared to what would happen to them.

After you find Helena, my mind reminds me.

"Where is my mate?" My twin glares at me at my question, and I debate dropping him, but the fucker will just fly if I do.

"Nice of you to join us, brother." Sneering, he shoves off my hold, and his own wings spring up.

"Where is my mate?" Clenching my teeth and my jaw, I push the words out.

"She went looking for our cousin and her friends." Colt lifts both hands in surrender when my body stiffens. "Beelzebub and Leviathan are with her. The fucking Archangel, as well as the damn Haltija, are there too."

"You let Leviathan get near her?" My roar echoes over the city as I fling myself at him.

We go down, all tangled limbs and wings, while I punch him in the face in rapid succession. Kicking with his legs, Colt hits my chest, sending me off him. We are both breathing hard when we face each other again. His eyes are burning in a fury, and he is barely holding onto his human form.

"The one that almost killed you was a jinn," Colt spits at me, his face twisted in anger. "For once in your life, ask questions before settling everything with your fists."

"I will ask questions after I find my mate."

I don't trust him.

Colt has always looked out for himself. He has no set of morals, no ideas of what is right or wrong. As long as it suits him and he gets on top, it's right in his book. We never saw face to face on anything. He accepts his place and sees it as something inevitable and granted. I don't. I want to make up my own mind, much to my father's displeasure.

"Well, you are in luck." My twin grins, looking over my shoulder, lifting a hand in greeting.

Flipping in the air and giving him my back, contrary to my better judgment, I look at the broken wall of windows in my apartment. The breath gets stuck in my throat when I see Helena leaning one shoulder on the side, watching up with her arms folded over her chest. That high, the wind is whipping her hair around her head, strands dancing around her beautiful face.

My entire body is shaking with the need to touch her.

I need to assure myself that she is real. That even though I wasn't there to protect her, she made it safely back. It's not me doubting her, not when she always doubts herself and the choices she makes. Yet, I've never met a person as compassionate or as a loving her. Even when she tries to hide it.

With my heart beating painfully hard and fast in my chest, my body coils up to spring at her so I can wrap her in my arms. Colt calls out my name in alarm when I shoot through the air. The fucker doesn't understand the need one has to hold his mate pressed to his skin. He can shout all he wants as long as I have Helena in my embrace.

The air rushes past my ears, but I don't look away from her. Keeping my gaze locked on hers, my breathing gets harsher the closer I get. Her green eyes flash, forcing me to blink, but a smile lifts her lips and I forget all about the weird light I imagined.

"Eric…" her voice covers me in chills.

She takes a step back, allowing me to land inside the apartment. I can see nothing but her. My whole purpose in life is centered on this woman. Helena looks me up and down before locking her gaze with me again.

She smiles, and all my blood rushes to my groin.

I reach for her, intending to tear her clothes off right here with Colt watching. I care about nothing apart from taking what is mine. Her smile grows when I take a step closer. I get yanked and thrown out the window before I touch her.

My furious roar rattles the building.

Chapter Thirteen

HELENA

I should've known that this woman was working with Mammon. Maddison's secretary, or assistant, never liked me. I based it all on the fact that she is obsessed with Eric, so it's kind of normal for her to hate my guts. Not really, but I can't say that it's strange. How I never thought that she might be involved is what pisses me off. I should've seen it.

A lot of things make sense the moment I realize that it's her voice. Not just the fact that she must be the reason the jinn, pretending to be Michael, found the demon sanctuary when the Holy ass kidnapped me. It's also the fact that she must be the reason Michael seemed to always be one step ahead of us. I also recognized her voice from my delirious states in that white room where they kept me. The female purring voice that grated on my ears, but I was too weakened to recognize at the time. Lauren has been tangled in this mess from the start.

Now, she will pay.

My steps slow down even when I feel the three men pound the pavement with their boots to reach me. My eyes are locked on Lauren's wide gaze. I'm not sure who she expected to see, but sure as hell it was not me judging by the stunned, slightly fearful look on her face. Narsi is still standing stiff and straight like a nutcracker, decorating the broken front door of that cursed building. She pays him no mind at all now.

My smile grows.

"Surprise." My voice bounces off cheerfully around us when I stop a few feet away from her.

She flinches.

"You need to get out of here." Snapping out of the shock, Lauren looks concerned when she steps closer to me. "Where are the rest? They'll be looking all over this city for you soon. It's not time yet for you to be walking around in the open." She looks me up and down, her face scrunching up in distaste. "But I must say you look perfect. I couldn't tell it was you for a second."

My eyebrows hit my hairline. I mean, I know I'm blonde, but does she really think I'm stupid enough to fall for this? Or she's hoping I didn't hear what she said to my sidekick. Come to think of it, Narsi is quiet as a church mouse, so unlike him that I flick my gaze in his direction. I frown when he keeps his face turned to Lauren, ignoring me.

"Oh, don't mind him." Lauren chuckles gleefully. "The wards that bitch Maddison placed around this building will hold anyone trapped like that until she releases them. We can just stay here and wait her out. She must come out at some point, and we might lure her away from her protection with you being here."

I'm still staring stupefied at this alternate reality I find myself in. What the hell is going on? Maybe Lauren went insane or something? None of this makes sense. I'm about to start asking questions when she looks over my shoulder, her face stretching in a wicked grin.

"Nice! They believe it's you!" her conspiratorial whisper makes me jerk back.

She thinks I'm someone else? Alarms blare in my head, my stomach dropping to my feet. The jinn flicking through faces, changing his appearance from one person to another is like a meteor hitting my head. My mind is spinning with this new development, the fact that the jinn can change into me and trick people into following them wherever they want. Why I find this strange after knowing for a fact that they impersonated Lucifer and Michael themselves is beyond me .*Maybe because you are no one special,* the voice in my head says snidely, but it's true.

I'm nothing special.

"Helena, you okay?" Raphael stops next to me, watching me warily.

"Yeah." I can only imagine what the three of them are thinking right now.

Now is neither the place nor time to get into explanations, and I can't look away from Lauren.

"What was that then, little girl?" Leviathan sneers, pointing at the uneven, cracked street, and I want to punch him to shut him up.

"I thought Lauren was going to get hurt." Keeping my face impassive, praying I can pull this off, I glance at the fallen in question. "The Trowe was acting strange. This is Maddison's assistant by the way."

"I did expect the worse." Lauren presses a hand on her chest, blinking at Leviathan.

My stomach churns, and I grind my teeth. If I didn't hear and see her for myself the last few minutes, I would've actually believed her. Beelzebub narrows his eyes, looking from me to Lauren a second before Leviathan does the same. My heart skips a beat. I don't know why, but deep in my soul, I know that if we just keep up this charade, we will finally be one step ahead of Mammon and the jinn. Wracking my brain to find something to say to keep this blowing in my face, I come up with nothing.

"Nice to see you again, Lauren." Raphael's voice jolts me from my panic. "I'm glad you are safe."

"Yeah, well…" Lauren pushes her breasts up, looking down her nose at him. In other words, her usual attitude. "It's not thanks to your brother Michael, that's for sure."

"Why is the Haltija frozen?" Beelzebub rasps, still not looking convinced that everything is okay.

"Maddison has strong wards." It's Raphael that answers him, and I see Lauren zero in on him with calculation in her eyes.

Oh no, you won't, bitch, I think to myself. Lauren might think everything is working out for her, but she will be in for a nasty surprise real soon. I feel Raphael's eyes on me, and I lock my gaze on his. His yellow eyes flick between mine, and I try my best to tell him something is wrong without being obvious about it. Seeing the golden glow blink once and a hard look entering his usually soft gaze almost makes me cheer. The Archangel turns to the two fallen, and I notice a look passing between the three of them. I can only hope Raphael understood me.

"Come, Maddison will release him when she sees it's us." Raphael turns his back on all of us, striding across the street.

Beelzebub and Leviathan are stiff around me, but Lauren is practically bouncing in her shoes. I follow Raphael, the sound of my heartbeat deafening in my ears. After staying alive all this time, Maddison and my friends, not just us, can get hurt or killed if this backfires. Is it worth risking their lives for this? What if Lauren doesn't know anything more than us? What if it's her playing us and this whole thing is a trap?

I have no time to work myself into more panic because Raphael whistles softly and, in no time at all, Maddison's face pops up in the shadows past the open door. A sigh whooshes out of me when I see her mane of red curls and unnaturally blue eyes come into view. The fear that she may not be as okay as Raphael said she was must've been subconsciously eating at me. I have to force my feet to stay planted so I don't rush for her.

"Helena?" Maddison's eyes glow that eerie light, and she looks me up and down. "Where is Eric?" She doesn't come closer or acknowledge the others, although her gaze flicks to Lauren for a second.

"He got hurt, so he is in a safe place right now." I'm unwilling to say where with Lauren here. "We came to get you guys there, too."

"Raphael?" Maddison finally looks at the Archangel. "I see you are back."

"Yes, it was not a visit as I expected." Taking a step to the side, he gives Maddison a clear view of all of us. "I couldn't tell who was who. Luckily, I can assure you that the four of us are who we say we are."

Maddison gives all of us a quick look before doing a double take on Lauren when Raphael's words get their point across. He said who the four of us are since Narsi is trapped. But it's five standing at Maddison's door, counting Lauren.

Lauren must've got his meaning too because she turns to flee, but Beelzebub and Leviathan already had her escape route cut off. She bounces off Beelzebub's broad chest, landing on her ass with an oomph. I blow out a breath in relief. No one jumped on us so we should be clear.

"If this is the real Helena, I have to tell you that even if I die today, I'll die laughing because I know that right this minute that arrogant fuck Eric is getting sliced up!" Lauren laughs in my face, and I'm already running so fast I can barely hear the shouts telling me to wait from behind me.

Oh, dear God, no! Eric!

Chapter Fourteen

HELENA

We are no longer hiding or trying to be stealthy. I've never run this fast in my life even when I had murderers going after my head. But, no matter how hard I push myself, Eric seems too far away. I will never reach him in time, and I can only pray that Colt will be strong enough to hold on until we get back. My feet are barely touching the ground as I pump my arms. That anger, the power that shakes the earth under my feet, churns inside me, but thankfully doesn't rattle the city so I can keep my feet under me. A shrill shriek comes from my mouth when arms wrap around my waist, lifting me in the air.

"I got you!" Hearing Leviathan of all people cuts of the second scream that was building in my chest.

"Faster!" I yell to be heard over the rushing wind.

The whooshing sounds of a couple more pairs of wings make me twist my head around. Raphael and Beelzebub are right behind us, their faces set in determination. Lauren must've gotten away if both of them are here. I can't find it in me to be upset about that when all I can think of is Eric, unconscious and surrounded by Mammon's lackeys and jinn.

"Lilith's daughter has Mammon's bitch." Leviathan grunts from above me and my face snaps up to look at him.

Leviathan acts aloof and arrogant, and most of the time, he just looks like he wants to murder everyone, but it's times like this when I'm reminded how perceptive the fallen is. I can't claim to know or understand any of them, so it's this moment I decide to cut him some slack. We all deal with our own bullshit, and unless I know everything about him, I should stop being as judgmental as those that judge me based on who my parents are instead of who I am.

I say nothing, but my fingers tighten where I'm clinging to his arms in gratitude. His piercing blue eyes snap to my face, and he holds my gaze for a long moment before jerking his head once in a nod. I guess me and the dragon came to some truce or something. Whatever it is, it makes me feel a little better at least. I can't dwell on it for long because I recognize the buildings under us. We are close to Eric's apartment, and all my focus turns on finding the building in question. My body sags in Leviathan's arms when I see it.

"Look!" Pointing frantically, I'm vibrating in his hold. "He is awake!"

I can't believe my own eyes. Eric is flying in front of our eyes, heading right for the penthouse. I want to laugh and cry from joy at seeing him awake and alive. That's until I see Colt right on his heels, gunning for him. Like two giant birds, they split the air like arrows. My body stiffens at the sight, and I feel Leviathan's muscles turn to granite under my fingers. Why is Colt chasing Eric like he wants to hurt him? They are still far enough away that it'll take us a few moments to reach them.

Leviathan doubles his efforts, his wings lashing the air with a vengeance so we can move faster. I stare at the scene unfolding before us, my eyes burning from the wind that's slapping my face. Holding my breath when Eric disappears inside his home, I pray that he and Colt don't hurt each other too much by the time we get there.

That should've been the least of my worries.

Someone else is inside the apartment, but I can only see a slight movement of an arm at the corner. Eric lands inside, reaching for whoever is there, when Colt nears the car-sized hole in the broken windows. Instead of landing as well, Colt doesn't slow his speed. Wearing off, he only grabs hold of Eric's wing, wrenching him out of the apartment and flinging him like a doll in the air.

I don't breathe.

An enraged roar splits the air a moment before Colt loses control of his direction. His body hits the side of the building, taking out a good chunk of it before following the debris to the ground. From the corner of my eye, I see Raphael tuck his white wings next to his body and shoot straight at Colt. I hope he reaches him in time.

Eric flips ass over head a couple more times before righting himself. He has changed his human form, and his double horns glint in the moonlight. His amber gaze locks on Colt, and a shiver goes up my spine from the rage in it. To my shock, he looks away from the target of his anger and focuses again on the apartment. Bile rises in my throat because as he nears it, I already know what I'm going to see.

I can't look.

"Eric!" Instead of looking at the jinn I know is in the apartment, I scream for my mate. "Eric, stop!"

"Shadow!" Beelzebub's bellow is much louder than mine.

Eric's head snaps in our direction, his burning gaze landing on me like he knows I'm here. The stillness in his body is unnerving. Even his wings stop their movement where he hovers in the air. He looks like a predator ready to pounce. Very slowly, his head turns to look at the apartment windows and I finally turn to see as well.

I'm standing at the center of the broken glass, my hair flying with a mind of its own around my head. It's perturbing to see yourself, your exact copy, staring at you with an evil smile. Eric and Colt are twins, identical for that matter, but I still notice little things that set them apart. Not counting the wicked smile and gleam in the eyes of my doppelganger, I can't even tell the difference.

"It's a jinn!" I shout at Eric, pointing at the disturbing copy of myself.

Leviathan stops close to him, still keeping enough distance to bolt out of here if Eric attacks. Not that I'll blame him. I wouldn't know who to believe either if I was in his place. He doesn't know what happened and that I personally brought all of them here. Since he knows me too well, Eric might try to kill us all. It's not like I knew I could bring fallen from Hell to the human realm with me. Not until I tried. So there is no way my mate knows.

"I got him." Raphael jars us all from our stare down, holding a banged-up Colt in his arms. "Unless any of you are planning to fight the jinn, I suggest we go back to the warded safe house. We need to make a plan so we can handle this better. Being on the defense is not the solution to our problems, and that's exactly what they want to keep us."

I think nothing could've convinced Eric more on who the copy is than the Archangel. Raphael's eyes soften, kindness, sorrow, and compassion mingling in his gaze when it lands on me. I don't doubt I look disturbed by seeing myself as another person, so it must be visible on my face. At least he doesn't look at me with pity. I'll take it.

"Stay away from my mate, fucker," Eric snarls, but I can tell he doesn't mean it.

The tension leaves my body, and I almost slip through my mate's arms when Leviathan hands me to him. Pressing my face to his neck, I breathe in his scent, swallowing the lump in my throat. Eric tightens his arms, squeezing me harder to his body as he follows the rest back to the only safe place.

The place where I was held prisoner.

Chapter Fifteen

HELENA

Clutching Eric with all my might, I want to find a way to crawl under his skin so deep and irreversible that no one will ever be able to take him away from me. I've never considered myself clingy, or needy for that matter, but damn if I don't feel all of that right now, and more. Obviously, I keep my mouth shut. The last thing I want is to come off like some psycho stalker. Let's all pretend that I'm not sucking in lungfuls of air, sniffing his skin like it's the only thing keeping me alive.

Eric doesn't mind. I mean, the guy is possessive and has his own quirks when it comes to me, so I guess we do make a weird, creepy, perfect couple. He kisses the top of my head, rubbing his cheek on it like a cat, but I'm the one that almost purrs from the affection. The five-o-clock shadow on his face catches strands of my hair, pulling gently on my skull with his movements. Tears are still leaking from the corners of my eyes, and luckily, the wind pelting us dries them faster than they flow so no one can see them. Eric can feel them on his skin, however, and his arms tighten reassuringly. I can't wait for us to get to the safe house so I can search everywhere on his body to make sure there is not a scratch on him. Only then will I be able to breathe again.

"Why are we headed this way…" Eric's words are cut off by a blinding flash of light splitting the dark, night sky.

I'm blinded for a second, my fingers digging into Eric's shoulders when his body jerks back and we go pirouetting down towards the ground. Shouts from above and a furious roar curdle the blood in my veins. Whatever that thing is, I hope it didn't hit any of the other guys, but that concern is left for later because very soon the two of us will end up splattered on the ground. We keep falling from the sky.

My body is yanked to a stop when Eric finally finds his control, his wings flapping the air with powerful sweeps. Breathing through my nose, I push down the bile that rises in the back of my mouth, still keeping my eyes closed in hopes the dizziness will go away.

"Hel, you okay?" Eric's deep voice vibrates through me, much more profound than his normal one, and that's oddly reassuring.

Whatever is coming for us, they'll have a pissed off double-horned demon to deal with at least. A very familiar roar makes me shiver. Well, a pissed off demon and a dragon from Hell too, it seems. There is no mistaking the sound Leviathan makes in his dragon form.

"I'm fine." My words sound strained, but I finally blink my eyes open. "What the hell was that?"

"We've got company." The muscles under my fingers are bunching up and jumping from Eric's anger. I squeeze his shoulders reassuringly. It's not like we haven't dealt with messed up situations like this before.

I mean, how bad can it be, right?

The spots dancing in front of my eyes disappear, and I

lift my face up to see what attacked us. Eric is still hovering in the same place where we stopped our downfall. I thought he was giving me time to gather my wits.

He wasn't.

I tighten my grip on him when I see the night sky ripped open like someone has taken a knife and opened the belly of the beast. White light is pouring out of it, but it's somehow centered just under the open slash. Me and Eric are hidden in the darkness, while the other four men are caught in the net of the light. Like black spots, the four of them are visible, Leviathan more than the rest since he is a fire-breathing dragon. His large head is lifted up while he belches flames at the gash in the sky. The light glitters and shimmers around them, and it takes a moment for me to accurately see what is happening.

That's when I notice them.

Angels in golden, gleaming armor with all sorts of weapons are streaking through the light, slashing and hacking at our friends. Not just at the two fallen and at Eric's brother, no. They are cutting at Raphael as well, even more so.

"Eric move!" Wincing when one large sword slices at Beelzebub's arm, I wiggle in Eric's arms. "We gotta help them. Don't just stand there!"

"I'm looking for a way in," he snaps through clenched teeth, and I see that he is not just hanging out here to stay out of it.

We've been moving slightly left and right while he is searching for an opening in the net of light. Instead of being an idiot and arguing like always, I start looking through it as well, trying to help him out. Colt gets kicked in the chest, and I watch his body fly back, passing through the light and disappearing in the darkness.

"We can pull them out!" Pointing frantically at the place I saw Colt last, I'm vibrating with the need to do something. "Colt just got kicked out of it!"

Eric doesn't wait to be told twice. Pulling me closer to his body, he shoots in the air, aiming at the closest of them. I watch Beelzebub swing his tree-trunk arms, sending angels flying all around him. His shirt and pants are ripped wherever they've been cut with their weapons. We stop just before the light begins, waiting on the edges to get a chance to pull him out. Eric jostles me up his chest to free one of his arms and reaches for the light. As soon as his fingers touch it, it sends us flying backward, hard. Eric's wings bow outward, and he manages to stop us not far from it.

Okay then, we can't touch it. Well...my eyes roam around the light. It calls to something in me, and I can feel its warmth. Mind spinning with options, I can only think of one other thing to try.

"Eric, I'll give it a go. Bring us closer." He stiffens at my words, and it pisses me off straight away. "Unless you have a better idea, stop being an overprotective ass and let me attempt it. Do you want them to die in there?" I glare at him.

"She has a point." Colt's voice scares the shit out of me. I didn't hear him come up next to us.

"You okay?" I crane my neck to see him. Eric grunts at my question and I see him looking at me with his eyebrow raised.

"I'll be as good as new in an hour." Colt chuckles in Eric's face, and I want to punch him. "So, what are we doing?"

"I need to pull them out of there since you two can't." I sound so confident one might think this is something I've done a thousand times.

I have no idea what I'm doing. Or if it'll work.

"Okay, let's do it," Colt agrees immediately, making Eric growl again.

I elbow him in the ribs.

"Let's go!" Wiggling around, I press my back firmly to Eric's chest, trusting that he won't drop me. "Bring me as close as you can."

"I have your back," Colt adds. He can be sweet like that sometimes.

Holding my breath, I wait for Eric to make up his mind. We are both stubborn as mules, and I know if I keep pushing him, he will resist it more. So, I stare at the battle happening in front of my eyes, not breathing. There is no time to waste, I can tell they won't be able to hold on for much longer. Just when I'm about to scream in frustration, Eric moves.

Releasing the breath I was holding, as soon as we reach the border of the light, I close my eyes and jab both arms through it, reaching for Beelzebub.

Chapter Sixteen

HELENA

While most things are piled up against me in life, there are a few that work in my favor. As soon as my fingers tangle in Beelzebub's shirt, I can tell this thing is one of the good ones. I pull as hard as I can, the guy is as large as a truck, and Eric flaps his wings hard, aiding me. It's like dragging someone out from a quicksand. My arms are shaking and sweat trickles down the sides of my face by the time the fallen pops out of the light trap. Beelzebub keeps swinging, so Eric yanks me away, just as Colt clocks him in the jaw to snap him out of it.

"Halt!" Colt roars in his face, and Beelzebub's red eyes swing wildly between all of us.

"Fuck!" He rubs his face angrily. "That thing fucks with your head."

"Chat later." I nudge Eric with my elbow, again. "The other two are still trapped."

Eric takes me around closer to Raphael. Smart on his part since Leviathan is a freaking dragon and, right now, I don't even want to think about how I'm going to pull him out. At least the angels don't pay any attention to what's going on outside the light. I frown at the thought, but we are already hovering near Raphael. The Archangel is truly a sight. He flips and turns, his body moving gracefully through the air while he is using not just his limbs, but his wings as well, to send those attacking him flying through the air.

They keep coming back.

Now that Colt and Beelzebub are not there, the angels are swarming Raphael and Leviathan. The dragon is a lot larger and keeps breathing fire, so he is somewhat holding his own. Raphael, on the other hand, is not doing very well. And that's when I notice what he is doing. While the angels are going for the kill, Raphael is only defending himself without doing much damage to any of them. The stupid Archangel will get himself killed because he doesn't want to hurt his kind. I'm going to kick him when all of this is over.

"I'm ready," I tell no one, in particular, not looking away from Raphael.

Eric grunts.

I mean, of course, he does. Why would he use words like an average person when he is sulking because I'm putting myself in danger, regardless of the fact that no matter what I do, or where I go, danger follows me like a bad smell. Ignoring him, I ready myself to grab hold of Raphael. He is not as lucky as Beelzebub. Maybe because he is not as thick as the fallen, the Archangel's leaner body moves a little faster. I have to reach in and snatch my hands back quite a few times, as well as wait for him to come closer to the edge of the light, until I can get a hold on him. Eric is vibrating in tension, and I can feel his body twitching on my back. If I don't grab Raphael soon, I just know Eric will move me away from here.

Telling myself I'll apologize for it later, I grab hold of one of Raphael's wings, twisting my fingers in as many feathers as I can, and I pull with everything in me. Eric yanks back with all his strength, sending all three of us flying back in the air. Raphael's roar splits the sky and thunder cracks above our heads. His angry and pained golden gaze lands on me, and it makes me gulp.

"I had to get you out of there, Raphael." He keeps glaring, and to my horror, I realize I'm holding handfuls of his feathers in my hands.

Not looking away from him, I unclench my stiff fingers, releasing the soft white feathers to drift slowly in the air. A few are sticking to my sweaty palms, so I peel them away slowly, flinging them wherever they fall. Hopefully, he won't attack. Right?

Colt snorts.

Raphael swings his gaze on him, and I can finally take a breath. Damn, the Archangel is scarier than a demon when he is pissed. There was nothing human in his golden eyes while they were locked on me. It drove home the point that no matter how kind and sweet Raphael is, he is still not human. He is high in the food chain in Heaven.

Heaven!

"Why didn't you leave the trap, Raphael?" Anger burns through me, replacing the fear from a second ago. "Since Eric can't touch the light, I'm assuming it's Heaven's light. What the hell were you doing fighting there instead of getting them out?"

"I couldn't leave, either." A muscle jumps in his jaw, but at least he is not looking like he wants to kill me anymore. "I told you Heaven is in chaos as well. I'm not sure how many of those are real angels."

Eric jerks like someone slapped him. Right, he doesn't

know yet everything that's been going on while he was hurt and unconscious. We can explain later, after we figure out how to get Leviathan. My eyes go over Raphael's shoulder to look at the dragon. I can barely see the black scales of his body from the golden armor surrounding him. I don't think he has long. We need to get him out now.

"Umm…guys." Pointing a finger, I show them what I'm looking at. "We need to get him out."

"You can't reach him." Eric, always the helpful one, points out, and I put everything in me when I elbow him this time.

"Thanks, Mr. Obvious. Now tell me how it can be done." Glaring at the other three, I make sure they all know how serious I am. "Because I'm not leaving here without him."

"Hand her over, Eric." Beelzebub comes closer, reaching for me, but Eric zips away.

"Stop for a second, monster boy." We so don't have time for Eric throwing a tantrum right now. "Let's hear his idea, and we will see if it's good, okay?"

"I'm not handing you over." His arms tighten, emphasizing his words.

"Okay, fine." I snap at him. "You can hold me, but let's hear what he has in mind." I wave Beelzebub closer.

All three of them move around us again.

"Remember when we were going for the portal, and Narsi fell off of Colt's back?" Beelzebub's face looks impassive, but his red eyes are drilling holes in mine. "You caught him by sitting with your knees on my back."

That is so not what happened that day. The Trowe didn't fall; the Harpies snatched him off of Colt's back. And I definitely did not catch him. It was Colt that grabbed him before he hit the ground. I was sitting on Beelzebub's back on my knees so I could fight the Harpies off. My mind is whirling with what he is trying to say.

"You are the only one that can go in and out of the trap," Beelzebub continues, his eyes saying something totally different from his words. "You can sit on Eric's shoulders, and you'll be able to push more than just your arms through the light barrier. When you have a good hold, we will all pull the two of you out."

"No!" Eric's shout slices the air.

I pray for patience with Eric. No matter how much I miss him, I swear it only takes an hour to want to knock him out unconscious again. He can be so frustrating at times. But I'm done playing games, and the dragon is moving much slower with each passing second.

"Here is the deal, Eric." Looking over my shoulder, I lock gazes with him. "You'll either be the one to hold me, or you can hand me over to Beelzebub. Either way, I'm going after Leviathan, and unless you are planning to fight me, you need to make up your mind right now. He doesn't have much longer, and I will not let him die after bringing him here while he was protecting both of us." And because I can, as well as because I'm pissed off at him, I have to make a jab. "All that while you were hurt, unconscious, and unable to fight by my side."

A low blow, I know.

Eric's arms stiffen around me, and I see the shutters dropping behind his eyes. My heart hurts for saying that to him like it was his fault, but I see no other option if Leviathan is to stay alive. I'll have to find a way to make him understand why I said it after we all get out of here. My stomach flip flops, knowing things will get worse between us before they get better. I just hope we are stronger than this and get through it.

Eric doesn't say a word, but he doesn't hand me to Beelzebub either. I see that as a good thing and push the worry to the back of my mind. Holding my body stiff, I allow him to move me around before lifting me over his head. Grabbing hold of his larger horns, I swing my legs around, straddling his neck. He shudders but doesn't say anything. Wrapping my shins around his torso, I hold myself stiff while he flies as gently as he can towards the trap. As soon as he gets on the side where Leviathan is still fighting off the horde of angels, I realize I can't overthink this. If he suspects what I'm planning, he will get me out of here before I have time to blink.

With that in mind, I watch the dragon flip his tail, his head sending angels flying away from him. This is going to hurt like a bitch, but there is no time like now to go ahead with Beelzebub's plan. I just hope Eric doesn't kill him in the meantime. My legs go limp around Eric a second before I hear Beelzebub's shout.

"Now!"

I fling myself away from Eric with my feet on his chest, sail through the light, and land in the middle of the back of a pissed off dragon.

Chapter Seventeen

HELENA

Leviathan roars. Fire bursts from his wide, open jaws, sharp teeth as long as my forearm glinting in the light. My heart jumps in my throat and lodges itself there. The dragon starts bucking, doing his best to get me off him. He has no idea what landed on his back. As far as he knows, it could be one of the angels. One thing I'm grateful for is that you can't hear any sound from outside the light barrier. I'm sure Eric has Atlanta shaking from his fury right now. I almost topple over when the dragon jerks to the side, so I leave all thoughts of a pissed off mate for now. I need to survive first if I want to deal with him later.

Scrambling on Leviathan's back, I push my way up by grabbing hold of his scales. I think his fire will burn me, the ones flickering in short bursts on his spine, but to my relief, they don't. They lick at my skin every time my hand nears them, but thankfully, I only feel slight heat. The angels haven't noticed me yet either, so that's a big plus. When I reach his long, snaking neck, I pause. How the hell am I planning to get him to listen to me? As far as I

89

know, Leviathan in his dragon form doesn't like me much. Not after I sliced his nose open. I tighten my hold on his scales when he drops a few feet down all of a sudden. Shit, he is getting tired, and I can see where swords and blades have sliced him open. Black blood is trickling from his wounds.

"Here goes nothing."

Without overthinking it, mumbling under my breath about the stupid jinn and that idiot Mammon, I inch up the dragon's weaving neck, using my arms and my thighs. As bad as it sounds, I'm kind of glad he is occupied with fighting off the angels, or I have no doubt he would be picking me out of by now. When I get as high as I'm comfortable with, I cling as tight as I can and start yelling at him.

"Leviathan!" My voice gets lost in the light, as if the damn thing is soaking it up.

Shit! There is no way he will hear me.

Wracking my brain on what else to do, I scream in pain when one of the angels opens a gash in my thigh. That hurts like a bitch. Tears burn my eyes, and I can feel my thigh throbbing while my pants get soaked with my blood. The angels get into a frenzy like piranhas at the sight of me bleeding. Oh God, this is bad. This is really, really bad. Like the stupidest idea I've ever head. Worse than going to Hell.

The dragon roars again, and to my shock, he stops trying to shake me off. Did he see it's me? Please God let him see it's me so we can get the hell out of here. Fire bursts from Leviathan's jaws, roasting all the angels close to me. It gives me hope that maybe, just maybe, we are not screwed. He turns his massive head to the side and his large eye zeros in on me. His vertical pupil expands and retracts as he keeps watching me. Since he can't hear me, I release the hold with one hand and start pointing at the edge of the barrier like a crazy woman. There is nothing else I can think of to do.

Luckily for me, Leviathan moves closer to the edge. We hover there for long moments while he fights off the new group of angels that got close enough to slash at him. My mouth goes dry when I get a closer look at them. There is no expression on their faces, not even the inhuman one I saw on Raphael when I pulled him out. Their eyes are empty, and all of them are fighting like one person. It's the closest explanation I can come up with. One person that has multiplied and all the copies are moving in sync with the original.

Leviathan dips again for a few feet, and I jolt, yelping as I tighten my hold. I lose sight of the angels, but my mind is swirling with possibilities. Can it be that simple? Like if we find the one that they are all mimicking, all of this will stop? Because it doesn't look like we will be able to get out of here. Every time Leviathan nears the edge of the light trap, they swarm us more. No, getting out is not an option.

We need a plan B.

"Where is Waldo." I chuckle crazily under my breath.

If this idea is a bust, we are as good as dead, I think. But I can't think of anything else, and it's not like I can have a chat with the dragon. He is busy keeping the angels away from us, and even if I scream, he won't hear me. I abandon the idea of getting through the barrier and start looking at the angels.

They come in groups, but the longer I watch them, the more I notice that they move only on one side at a time. I have no idea what that means, but I'll take it. Straining my eyes, I try to see beyond the group attacking us now. There is the second group just floating there behind them, waiting. When Leviathan sends fire at the attackers, they bolt back, then the second group comes at him. A peculiar thing happens. One from the second group joins the first instead of coming at us with his buddies. Thinking I imagined it out of desperation to survive, I keep watching. Three times they switch places, and three times the one I've been watching switches groups and never attacks.

That's the motherfucker I'm going to stab.

Still dumbfounded that I was actually right, I start slapping Leviathan on his scales to get his attention. When he locks his eye on me, I point frantically at that one angel I've been eyeing. Praying that he sees what I see, I hold my breath when he starts turning. All I need is to get close enough so I can slice at him. Sliding my hand at the small of my back, I grab hold of my dagger. My wounded thigh has gone numb, I can barely feel that leg, but whatever. If I'm wrong about this one angel, both of us are going to die here anyway.

No matter how many times Leviathan tries to get close to that one, the others force him to move back. Like they are protecting him. It only firms my belief that if we get rid of that one, we might survive this. When a long time has passed, and we get close but not close enough, I throw caution to the wind. The moment Leviathan nears that one angel, I push off his neck and throw myself at him.

We both freeze, staring at each other wide-eyed, me shocked that I actually jumped that far to grab hold of him and I'm assuming he is in shock that he got busted. Anger darkens his features, and his face flickers, changing into the too beautiful face of a jinn, but I didn't risk my life to let this jerk kill me now. Still staring at his face, I pull back my arm, and as hard as I can, I shove the dagger in his chest. His mouth opens in shock, and a triumphant smile splits my face.

"Playtime motherfucker." I grin at him.

The light disappears with a pop, and a loud sound rushes to my ears. Roars, fights, curses, and the pissed off roar of a dragon reach my ears. I forget all about it when the jinn goes limp and puffs out of existence like he was never there. I plummet to the ground with a shout.

"Shit!"

Chapter Eighteen

HELENA

I get snatched in the air by Eric. I'm not at all surprised because I somehow know he will catch me. He always does, even when my feet are on the ground. He won't look at me, anger still simmering under his skin, but that's okay. We are all alive, and there is one less jinn around here. That's a good night in my book nowadays. Looking over his shoulder, I watch the flash in the sky. The light trap might be gone, along with the jinn, but the portal to Heaven is still gaping open like a beacon in the night. Will demons be able to go through it? Watching Eric's angry face from the corner of my eye, I'm not sure if I should ask. *Pick your battles wisely, Hel,* I tell myself, sighing.

"We are hard to miss in the air, guys." I still feel uneasy from the whole thing so I can't stay quiet. "We should go the rest of the way on foot, so we don't bring trouble there straight away. I know I can use a little break."

I haven't even finished talking when Eric descends. As soon as my feet touch the ground, he removes his arms from me and walks ahead of us. My heart hurts, and a lump forms in my throat. Blinking fast, I'm hoping the tears won't spill down my cheeks. I know I hurt him, so I shouldn't feel sorry for myself. I deserve him giving me the cold shoulder. A large hand on my shoulder pulls me out of my miserable thoughts. I expected Raphael or even Beelzebub. It's none of those two.

"Thank you." Leviathan looks uncomfortable, glaring instead of looking at me like I saved his life.

I did. But that's not important.

"Now, we are even." Smiling slightly at him, Eric's stomping falters ahead of us. "And you can't hold a grudge because I sliced your nose. That was an accident anyway. You know I have a kneejerk reflex."

"I have noticed." His thick lips twitch, and his glare deepens because, God forbid, he smiles at me or anything.

"Yes, Helena." Raphael's voice makes me look at the Archangel. "Thank you for saving all of us. I don't know how the others reacted, but all I wanted while I was trapped in there was blood. I was fighting the urge with everything in me, but it would've eventually won. You have my eternal gratitude."

"Don't thank me." Shuffling uncomfortably, I try my best not to look at Eric. "You guys should thank Colt." The man in question almost trips over his own feet, gaping at me in shock. "What?" Chuckling at his expression, I poke at the rip on my pants. Raphael healed it as soon as Eric caught me, so now only a tear in the fabric is a reminder of what happened up there. "If I didn't see you flying out of the light barrier, I never would've thought of pulling you guys out."

"Yeah, that was luck on my side." Colt looks like he swallowed a hot potato. I guess he is not used to praise. "One fucker got tangled with me while another kicked me in the chest. I think the contact with it allowed me to get out." He shrugs a shoulder.

"Whatever it was, I don't ever want to feel like that again." Raphael shudders, and the others grunt in agreement.

I feel bad for Raphael. The poor Archangel never asked for any of it, but his kindness to save my life and protect me got him tangled in all this mess. He tries not to show it, but I can see shadows in his yellow eyes when he thinks no one is watching him. I can't change my fate, can't change who my parents are. Still, out of everyone, I wish I can change things for him. I know deep in my heart he is a gentle soul, and it kills me that he is in the middle of my disaster of a life.

We continue in silence, each of us lost in our own thoughts. I keep glancing at Eric. He is withdrawn, his body stiff as a board. I'm surprised he doesn't break in half. Hurt and anger shroud him like a cloak, and I see shadows merging and emerging from his body with a mind of their own. I need to talk to him if he lets me, but not with everyone around. I'm going to corner him when we get to the safe house, hopefully without getting into another trap or fight by then.

When we near the building, Eric gets tenser, if that's possible. I mean, I'm not really happy I'm going back here, but obviously, neither is he. He inches closer to me, I'm sure not intentionally on his part. But I say nothing, soaking up his nearness and the heat coming from his skin when our arms brush against each other.

"This is the safe house?" he growls incredulously.

"It was the only place that we can erect wards strong enough to keep everything out." Raphael shrugs unapologetically.

There is nothing any of us can say to that, so we keep moving. I'm happy to see that my sidekick is not still frozen at the front of the broken door. I wasn't aware that it was sitting like a boulder on my chest until just now when I finally take a full breath. Poor Trowe had quite a hard time ever since I found him.

We stop at the bottom of the steps, unable to move up. Well, none of them can. I tested it, and there is nothing stopping me from going up to the door. Keeping my mouth shut, I wait along with them until Maddison shows up, partially hidden in the darkness of the hallway inside. Her eyes jump from one to the next before finally landing on me. She lingered on Eric for longer than the other three, but I'm the target of her scrutiny more than anyone else.

I can guess why.

"I'm not a jinn if that's what you are worried about." The smile I try to give her falls flat, so I give up on it.

"Right." Looking down her nose at me, her musical voice is like a warm hug. "It'll take more than that to convince me." She comes closer to the door, stopping right before the threshold.

Raphael and Eric open their mouths at the same time, but I lift a hand, stopping their words. None of them will convince her of anything. And I like to believe Maddison knows me better than I know her. Because I fell for a copy of her that the jinn showed us. Hopefully, she wasn't and will never be that unfortunate.

"The wards are stopping everything from entering your safe house, right?" Keeping my gaze on hers, I wait until she nods reluctantly. There is wariness in her eyes, but I can tell she will go for my throat if I'm not telling the truth. How the hell did we get tricked by her doppelganger is beyond me now that I'm looking at her. "Even jinn?" I need her to confirm it before I do anything.

"Yes." Her eyes narrow slightly on her perfect face.

Steeling my spine, I take the first step. I can hear Raphael suck in a startled breath behind me. Her eyes widen, but she doesn't move, so I take another, and another. When I reach the top, and we are almost face to face, her shoulders drop and she breathes deeply.

"Thank goodness!"

Chapter Nineteen

HELENA

"I can't believe we fell for it." Looking from Raphael to Eric, I voice the thoughts running through my head.

Even in this half-broken building, Maddison looks as prim and proper as ever. There is not a hair out of a place where the red curls fall over her shoulders. The air around her is like the first time I saw her. I have to lock my knees or I'll bend down and curtsy in her presence.

"None of us suspected jinn." Eric shrugs, still avoiding my gaze. "At the time, I was more focused on finding you than I was worried if she is acting like her old self."

We are following Maddison through the hallways, her footsteps much lighter than my tired stomping in the tiled floors. My whole body feels like one big bruise, and I want to collapse in a heap on the floor. The fact that I don't want to show weakness in front of Eric, mainly to prevent him from saying I told you so, is the only reason I'm still standing.

As I've said a few times, we are both stubborn.

"So, who else is here?" My question makes Maddison look back at me.

"Two of your hunter friends are here." She gives me her back again. "Imagine my surprise when they just came out of nowhere, speaking to me like we were old friends." Shaking her head, curls bouncing, her soft chuckle makes me smile despite my tiredness. "I thought I must have taken the wrong portal on my way back."

"Where were you anyway?" I thought everyone the jinn impersonated was held captive. Then I remember looking at myself through the broken windows of Eric's apartment and I shiver slightly.

"I went to speak to my mother." Eric snarls something, but Maddison shuts him up with a wave of her hand. "Keep your growls for your mate, Eric. I have no time for it. I saw my mother because I knew something was coming. I just didn't expect it to start while I was looking for advice."

"And did you?" When she turns her head and lifts a perfectly shaped eyebrow at me, I clear my throat. "Get advice, I mean."

We stop moving, and she is fully facing me now. The men stay mostly quiet, and I'm grateful. I have a splitting headache, and too much talking will make it worse. Maddison searches my face before her gaze flicks from me to Eric, who is standing a few feet away from me. A barely noticeable line forms between her eyebrows for a second, but thankfully she doesn't say anything about it.

"There is a time for talking." She grabs the handle of the door where we gathered around. "I think what all of you need is food and rest first."

My stomach releases a thunderous and embarrassing sound as if punctuating her words. My face heats up, and I avoid looking at all of them. When was the last time I ate? I can't remember, and that's very bad right there. Eric's gloomy aura thickens more, if that is possible. Maddison reaches for me, removing my fingers from my mouth. I was subconsciously chewing on my thumbnail, so I smile sheepishly at her.

"I will get someone to bring food, you can go see your friends in the meantime." Her blue gaze softens for a second before she pushes the door open for us and walks away.

I haven't taken a full step inside when a ball of energy slams into my legs and only Eric stops me from falling on my ass. He holds my hips while Narsi climbs up my body, and I can't stop the snort. The Trowe really is something.

"Mistress..." He keeps hissing, holding onto me with arms and legs like a monkey.

"Careful, you'll hurt her." Eric snarls from behind me, and warmth blossoms in my chest. Maybe I didn't screw up as bad as I feared.

"Calm down Narsi, I'm fine." Petting his head awkwardly, I finally look past him in the room.

George and Cass are watching me warily, their eyes bugging out of their skulls. My heart skips a beat when I see two of my old team, but I stop myself from saying anything. Why are they watching me like they've never seen me before? Is it because of Narsi? I know for a fact I haven't grown horns since the last time they saw me. A groan escapes me at the thought of horns. Looking over my shoulder only confirms it.

Eric is glaring daggers at everyone in the room and there are many gathered here that I've never met. His wings are tucked into his back but still visible over his shoulders. They stick out, crowding the hallway behind us. Two sets of horns are sticking proudly on top of my mate's head. To my team members, this might look like a demon is holding me hostage. The creepy, eyeless Trowe is not helping the matters much, either.

Taking a deep breath, I smile tightly at the hunters. "Hey, guys. Good to see you."

"Are you okay?" George lifts up, slowly keeping an eye on Eric. "You got back safe."

"So, it was really you at Sanctuary when the gate opened?" I try to take a step closer, but Eric and Narsi will have none of that.

"Yeah." Leaning his back on the wall behind him, George still looks poised, as if ready to fight. "That was definitely some trip, I'll say that much. We barely got away with our heads on our shoulders." He jerks his chin at Cass. She nods enthusiastically, confirming his words.

"The others?" Just thinking about Hector and Amanda clogs up my throat and I have to swallow thickly. Eric's hands tighten on my hips, and I sag against him.

"We have no idea." Dropping his tough act, George rubs his face. He looks like he's aged ten years since the last time I saw him. "This is so fucked up."

"You can say that again," Colt chirps before shouldering his way into the room. "All of you can stand as much as you want, but I need to fucking sit down. I'll watch my brother and the hunter play the dominance game from the floor." He plops next to Cass, giving her a wink. She shrinks away from him, even though he has no horns on his head.

"What are you talking about?" I frown at him, already angry that he is scaring my friend.

"The hunter can feel the mark my brother left on you, but his human brain can't process it for what it is. So, he is puffing up his chest like a peacock." Colt points at George, grinning like an ass. "My brother, on the other hand, is still pissed off at you, but just like a dog with a bone, he makes sure the hunter knows not to pee on his territory." He stabs a finger at Eric. "It's rather fun to watch. I just can't stand anymore. So, I took a front row seat."

My mouth hangs open, and Colt laughs in my face. Cass, my quiet and sweet friend, snorts ungracefully, slapping a hand over her mouth as her eyes go wider. Eric grumbles something about ripping Colt's wings off to teach him a lesson, and the other three roar a burst of laughter from the hallway. None of it shocks me as much as my sidekick.

"Leave Shadow alone!" Narsi hisses at Colt, baring his teeth, and if Eric weren't holding me, I would've dropped on the floor.

Chapter Twenty

HELENA

The food that they bring us gets devoured in less than five minutes. It makes me think back to how many times I've actually eaten since all this started. The more my powers settle in my body, the less hungry I feel. I haven't thought about food at all. Raphael was healing me while Michael, or the jinn pretending to be the Archangel, kept me in this very building. Then Eric said he was feeding me his energy when I went nuclear in Hell and lost a few days because of it. The more time passes, the less I have a need for it. It's a very unsettling thought on top of everything else, so I push it away.

"You didn't do anything to regret." Keeping my voice casual, I glance at Raphael.

He is sitting across from me on the floor, pushing the last couple of bites he has left around his plate. I don't need to hear it to know how he is feeling. The expression on his face and the shattered look in his yellow eyes tells me everything. He is disturbed because of the way they made him feel in the trap. I felt the same when I thought I'd have to fight

Michael. Standing against anything to do with Heaven didn't sit well with me. I think something inside me died that day in the Sanctuary when Michael told me I shouldn't have been alive. I kept my life, yes, but something fundamental changed inside of me that night.

"I know, Helena." Raphael smiles sadly. "It doesn't mean that what is happening is not bothering me a great deal. This should not have happened...none of it."

"Funny you say that." At his raised eyebrow, I shake my head, "I was telling Eric that we act like we have a choice in things, yet no matter what happens, it seems like the choices have been made for us a long time ago. Whoever is pulling the strings had this all planned out to the smallest detail." Raphael turns his full attention on me at that. "I told him that I will not play their games anymore. I have a theory, but it might be just grasping for straws at this point."

We are talking quietly, all of us sitting in a group at one corner of the room. Even Eric turns his brooding intent gaze on me when I speak those words. I can feel their eyes like a weight on my chest. Should I keep my mouth shut or voice my thoughts and get all of us killed with my assumptions? Regardless that I've had a few lucky guesses, I can't be sure that I'm right. As always, Eric can feel me faltering through the bond, and he comes to sit next to me.

"Tell us what is going on through that pretty head of yours, Hel." Eric still feels closed off, but he takes my hand between two of his. "None of us are your responsibility. We are all capable of making up our own minds and either agreeing or disagreeing with your ideas. As things stand right now, we are backed into a corner. Something has to be done." A buzz of agreements comes from all of them, but I still hesitate. I have too many souls on my conscious already, how many more can I take before I lose myself completely?

"Eric is right." Raphael nods slowly. "With Michael and Lucifer missing, the portals are not stable and are opening left and right, sometimes at random. The realms are merging and barely perceptive, but you can feel the rips in the fabric of life if you pay close enough attention." The fallen, Colt and Eric all nod at that, my stomach tightening at the solemn look on their faces. "It might've started with Mammon being his usual self, but this...this is past anything he could've planned or expected. He was being a pawn like the rest of us, although I'm not sure he knows it yet."

"I'm a big guy, Hel." George clenches his jaw, acting like he is not side-eyeing everyone warily. "I can make up my mind on what to do. But I need to do something. Running and hiding is not helping anyone, it's just delaying the day we all meet our end. We were born for this..." His hands are white knuckled in his lap. "You, too, because I don't give a shit what any of them say. You are a hunter, Hel, and one of the best damn hunters Heaven has ever seen, whether they want to admit it or not." He glares at Raphael, daring him to say something, but the Archangel simply nods, and tears prickle my eyes. "We are hunters, and it is our duty to protect humankind. From demons, yes, but angels too, especially if they are a threat. These jinns that are wreaking chaos are not even on the list of things I will hesitate to kill."

"They have enough of my blood to open tons of portals everywhere. In this very building, they took enough to last them a lifetime, if you remember." Raphael closes his eyes, and Eric growls low in his chest, but I didn't say that to remind them of my misery. "The jinn don't just have Michael and Lucifer." Blowing out a breath through puffed out cheeks, I pull my hand away from Eric and, spearing my fingers in my hair, I yank on it to clear the swirling thoughts. "My parents are missing too, from what we know. That's what I don't understand. Are they just collecting the most powerful entities? And if that's the case, why are Beelzebub, Leviathan, and Raphael still here? Why is Mammon running around unchecked and Lilith is not getting involved? Didn't you say you fought Gabriel in Heaven?" I stab a finger at Raphael. The more I talk, the more I feel like screaming in frustration. "Everything seems random, and it doesn't make any sense."

I told Raphael, George, Cass, Maddison, and Eric, since he was unconscious for some of it, everything that happened. Eric filled Maddison in on what she missed while we were dealing with the jinn impersonating her as well. So now it's in the open that they are sitting with the daughter of Satan himself, but none of them has left so far. I guess that's a good thing. George's speech about me being a hunter was for that reason, I think. I'm grateful to him, but it still doesn't make me feel better. I've worked myself up into a frenzy, and the ground shudders under us.

"Hel, breathe." Eric grabs my face between his palms, forcing me to focus on him. "Tell me what you are thinking. What do you think you should do?" He is back in his human form and the dark green of his eyes pulls me back from the anger and panic.

"She is much stronger than when I last saw her," Maddison says, speaking for the first time since she told us to eat when the food was brought over. "It takes a long time to develop dormant or suppressed powers."

"That's another thing, too." Pulling out my dagger, I twirl it in my hand. "Ever since I got the weapon, things started developing faster. Why on earth did a jinn give me this?"

"Because they don't want you dead." We all look at Maddison when she drops the bomb. "What? Are you all daft? I don't think even Satanael and Zadkiel knew what she was going to become. You, Helena, were given the weapon because they needed your powers to manifest. I'm not sure they knew how fast that will happen, maybe they thought they'll have you in their clutches by then. Whatever the jinn are planning, you are the key to it. A patient zero if you will."

"And now they have a carbon copy of me walking the streets." My heart is thumping so hard against my ribs, it's painful.

Chapter Twenty-One

HELENA

"You are not helping." Eric snarls at Maddison, pulling me into his lap.

On the bright side, it looks like he doesn't remember that he is upset with me for risking my life to save Leviathan. Her face when she gives me a satisfied, pointed look tells me that was her intention. Even in my panic, I can't stop my lips from twitching at how smart the woman is. It's little unnerving to think she can be a worse enemy than the jinn if she decides she wants to rule the realms.

Wiggling a little to get more comfortable in Eric's arms, I soak up his nearness. Surrounded by his body and scent, I am more centered and less freaked out. Running my hands over his muscled arms, I lean my head on his shoulder, trying to find the courage I need so I can say what is in my head. But I don't look at any of them, instead focusing on the floor.

"I keep thinking about every time I have been in the presence of a jinn pretending they are someone I know." Closing my eyes, I recall all instances, shivering involuntarily. "Out of all of them, the time when Eric was hurt is nagging at me the most." Eric stiffens, but I kiss his neck to show him I don't mean it the way he thinks. "Not because my mate was hurt, although that is a large part of it. The energy that they emit in order to trick us into believing they are who we actually see was off. I didn't think about it at the time, but Colt pointed it out. Leviathan confirmed it when he joined us before we had to fight Mammon and his horde to get out of Hell. They mimic what they think we are aware of. In the case of Lucifer, the jinn was bursting with seductive power, thinking that is how I felt it the first time I saw Eric's father. It was not, because Lucifer's powers were like I've touched a live wire when I met him. Same with Leviathan, the dragon hurt Eric but didn't make me feel like my body was burning and my skin was melting off my bones."

"What are you saying, Helena?" Maddison looks like she is trying to read my mind, her gaze so intent I can only glance at her and close my eyes again.

"I think they've been studying us for a while, way before any of this actually started. Not just our powers, or our physical appearance, but *us*. Watching and learning so they can replace us with one of themselves for whatever agenda they are trying to achieve. And then their plans got twerked. Now they seem like they are running out of time, and they are making mistakes. Or, so I think."

"Twerked how?" I tilt my head at Raphael's question so I can see him.

"Hector." A lump as big as a tennis ball forms in my throat, and I have to clear it twice. "I'm not sure what he knew or how I just know with everything in me that the reason he went looking for Eric specifically was because of it."

All of them burst into a heated conversation, spitting insults and arguing that the Order is power hungry and working against the reason it was created in the first place. My hunter friends get vocal, defending what we as hunters stand for. All of it is a distant buzz because Maddison is watching me like she finally sees me for the first time. I look back, not hiding from her penetrating stare. It's like she enters my mind and my body with ghostly fingers, poking and prodding without being invasive. I would've let her even if she was. Raphael and Eric were right. We are backed into a corner, and we either find a way out, or we are all screwed.

Everyone is now gathered around us.

"Silence!" Maddison didn't even raise her voice, but everyone snaps their mouth shut like someone presses the mute button on a remote control. "Go on." She nods at me.

Pursing my lips, I deflate like a popped balloon. I'm going to say my peice and they'll either laugh and call me crazy, or they'll think I'm narcissistic and leave my self-centered ass to deal with everything on my own. *You are backed into a corner, Hel. You can do this, and you have Eric,* I tell myself sternly because no matter what I know, I can always count on monster boy. He will stick by me through thick and thin, just like I would do for him. There is no doubt in my mind on that. He kisses the top of my head in encouragement, and the steady beat of his heart under my cheek is enough for me to speak.

"I thought it all started when the rogue demon raked its nails on my arm, taking my blood. Knowing what I know now, it started before that. Hector looked for Eric, hiring him to kill me before any of that happened. I think it was first because he knew something was coming, and second because he hoped that Eric would not be able to do it. I can't say for certain, even after Hector told us it was his plan all along." The entire room is deathly silent, prickling my nerves, but I push through my discomfort. "The feeling I have inside me, the one I call GPS for lack of a better word, started getting stronger and more persistent a month or two before Hector spoke to Eric. I never said anything, but the man who raised me knew me better than I know myself. I have no doubt he was aware something was up. So, he took matters into his own hands in hopes to protect me. As much as I want to be angry and hate him for what he did, that's one thing that Hector has always done. He has protected me to the best of his ability." Twisting my fingers in my lap, I look at all the faces around me. "I think that his actions are what pushed the jinn to start acting in a rush. Things were getting worse, yes, but not at this alarming rate. That night I met Eric is when, out of nowhere, Michael showed up at the Order wanting to kill me. It's just too much of a coincidence for me to not see it as a turning point. Because my parents were already missing at that time. I have no doubt jinn were planted in the Order, and at the same time others were out making deals with Mammon. The only thing missing was the human realm, and I think they want me so they'll have control of all three. I just have no idea how they are planning to use me."

You can hear a pin drop.

"I will eat their face!" Narsi bursts into a hiss from behind me, and I almost jump out of my skin.

Chapter Twenty-Two

HELENA

Eric swats the Trowe like a pesky fly and my sidekick bumps into the feet of those standing around us. If he didn't scare the crap out of me, I would've felt sorry for him. The creepy creature has the worst timing ever for everything he does. It's almost as if he is doing it on purpose.

"I agree," Raphael and Maddison say at the same time, and Leviathan snarls at the Archangel.

My eyebrows hit my hairline at the aggressive reaction from the fallen. It's not like Raphael argued with her. Maybe we are all just strung up tight and acting like everyone is against us. Oh, wait, they are.

"It makes a weird kind of sense," George says reluctantly, Cass nodding her head next to him like she can't stop it from moving.

If anyone understands what I was trying to say about Hector, it's my team. They grew up around the man as well, and they know how collected, kind, and protective he is. Hiring a hit on my head notwithstanding.

"We still have no plan on how to deal with this." Colt pushes the words angrily through clenched teeth.

"What? You don't like it when others are fucking with your life, brother?" Eric mocks him from behind me, and I elbow him in the gut.

"Really guys, now is so not the time for the two of you to go at it. Let's come up with a plan, and after that, you two can try to kill each other." Glaring at both of them, I pick up the dagger, waving it around. "Or I can stab you both, which might be faster."

"Now you know why I like her." Beelzebub slaps Raphael on the shoulder so hard he almost topples on the floor.

"Anyway…" Raising my voice to shut them up because I'm not Maddison and they don't take me as seriously, I continue. "What I'm saying is, I think Hector twerked their plans and the jinn felt the need to move faster. That's why we are seeing all the discrepancies and can keep up with them somewhat. But, even knowing what we know, they are always one step ahead. I think that's because they anticipate everything we do since we all act and react as expected. If we want to get a handle on the situation, we must act unpredictably. Or unlike ourselves. However you want to put it."

"Okay, what do we do?" George is first to jump on my crazy plan train.

"Hey!" Lifting both hands up, one still holding the dagger, makes everyone flinch back. Twisting my mouth, I put it in my lap, intentionally slow, and all the men glare at me. I ignore them. "That's all I got as far as plans go. I'm not a strategic mastermind here. Give me a target, and I'll kick its ass, I can't come up with detailed instructions on what we should do. I'm a spur of the moment kinda girl."

"For a start, we have Lauren detained and ready for

questioning." Maddison lifts up, straightening invisible wrinkles on her expensive clothing while the rest of us look like shipwreck victims.

At least we ate, and no one is trying to kill us here. There is always a silver lining if you look hard enough.

"I'll question her." Just the sound of Eric's voice can tell a deaf person why he shouldn't be the one doing any questioning.

"I think I can handle it, cousin." Sarcasm is dripping like molasses from Maddison.

I want to be like her when I grow up. I might have a girl crush watching her with admiration as she swings her hips, leaving the room like a Queen after gracing the peasants with her presence. Why can't I shut them up like she does? Is it a power of hers that does that? Because if it is, I want it! I see the fallen, the Archangel, George, and Colt watching me suspiciously, and I grin at them. Okay, I bare my teeth, but it does the trick, making their eyes turn to slits. I don't have to see Eric's face to know it's the same, I can feel him at the back of my head.

"Whatever it is that you are thinking, she-devil, don't do it," Colt says, obviously on team testosterone.

"I'm not thinking anything." Blinking innocently at him doesn't make any of them change their facial expression.

They watch me for a long moment, but eventually turn and start talking to each other. All humor leaves me, and I slump back in Eric's arms. I seriously expected them to call me crazy when I tell them what's been going through my head. Everything feels farfetched and based on guesses, but after saying it out loud, it only firms up my belief. I recall meeting Lauren earlier as well. We've never spoken directly and kept away from each other. Also, she's only seen me at times when I was freaked out because my world fell apart.

Acting unlike my usual self made her believe I'm my doppelganger. Can it really be that simple?

"If Maddison gets good intel on the jinn, I think I want to infiltrate their group." A squeak is ripped from me when Eric's arms tighten painfully around me. "Just hear me out, please."

"Let her speak, Shadow." Beelzebub scowls at Eric.

"Last time you said that, my mate was on Leviathan's back, fighting off a horde of jinn," Eric snarls.

"Well, technically it was one jinn," I add helpfully, making Leviathan snort and shake his head. "What? It was only one. And you are welcome."

"The only people the jinn are impersonating without being missing is you and Maddison." Eric grinds through a clenched jaw. "You are not going, and that is final."

"Unless you want me dead, I don't see what else we can do, Eric." Raphael's mouth moves, surely readying himself to add something that will not help me, so I keep talking. "I'm tired of running, fighting, and always looking over my shoulder. If we are to do something unpredictable, I can't think of anything more drastic than that. They'll never think I'm crazy enough to just waltz in between them."

"It could work." Raphael looks shocked at his own words.

"We will talk about this no more!" Eric is done playing nice.

I shriek like some damsel in distress again when he jumps off the floor with me still in his arms. His body is vibrating in anger that not even I can soothe right now, probably because I'm the cause of it. People part when he strides through the room, and I hear Narsi hissing something from behind us. My sidekick whimpers at the same time when Eric's body jerks. The loud thump confirms my fears that my mate just kicked the Trowe. Poor little creature. If I weren't in so much trouble, I would've been upset on his behalf. But I have to make Eric see this is the only way to beat the jinn at their own game. Looking at the storm on his face, I press my lips tight and start riling myself up for a fight.

A fight monster boy is not going to win.

Chapter Twenty-Three

HELENA

I sit stiff as a board in Eric's arms while he stomps through the hallways of the building. Anxiety from being in this place is pushing to the front of my mind, but I have so much other shit to deal with, it's easy to ignore it. Eric's caveman attitude is not helping one bit with any of it, and I think I'm at the end of the rope on my sanity.

He shoulders a door open and slams it shut with his foot the second we enter the room. Leaping out of his arms, I whirl around, slamming my hand on my hips. Wincing when the hilt of the dagger still clutched in my hand hits my hipbone, I grimace, sliding it to the small of my back.

"Are you trying to punish me, Hel?" Eric looms over me, his green eyes burning with anger and pain. "Is that what this is?"

"Punish you?" Taking a step back like he slapped me, I stare at him incredulously. "Why the hell would I want to punish you, monster boy?"

"I was reckless." Snarling, he starts pacing in front of me, yanking on his hair with both hands. "I didn't think of you, or your safety. Getting myself hurt and leaving you to fend for yourself in the middle of Hell with jinn running loose all over the realms and Mammon at our gates." I open my mouth, but he keeps rambling. "Instead of being the shield in front of you; I added to the weight on your shoulders, while my estranged brother fights by your side. I don't blame you for seeing me as weak. I've always been reckless, but this time I pushed way beyond what's acceptable."

Watching him pace, I frown, chewing on my lip.

"Acceptable to whom?" When he keeps mumbling and pulling on his hair, I can't help the snort that escapes me. "Yo, monster boy. Acceptable to whom?"

"What?" I'm thankful he stops because I am getting dizzy. The confusion on his handsome face almost makes me laugh.

"You said you were reckless beyond the acceptable limits. I wanna know who is the one that accepts them so I can apply to increase my limit."

Eric glares.

"Listen." Coming closer to him, I take his hand. "It's not me punishing you, it's you punishing yourself for something out of your control. It wasn't your fault that you got hurt." He tries to yank his hand away, but I'm having none of that, so I tighten my hold, digging my nails in his skin. "Eric, stop. It's not me blaming you for anything. You are blaming yourself, and all for nothing, I'll tell you that right now. Do you have any idea how badly I wanted you to wake up?"

"I shouldn't have been a deadweight in the first place." He is still snarling, but at least he is not trying to pull away.

"You didn't ask for it, and neither did any of us when we got hurt. That's why we must do this. I must do this." I'm praying he will understand so I don't have to push him away to do it. Because whether he agrees or not, my mind is already made up. "The longer we wait, the stronger the jinn will become. We can't let that happen. Did you look around on our way through Atlanta? I haven't seen any humans since we got back from Hell, and this world belongs to them. Not to the angels, not to the demons... and most definitely not to the jinn."

The green darkens in Eric's eyes as he keeps his gaze locked on mine. He doesn't say anything, but I can tell that he is finally listening, so I keep pushing, hoping that he will see reason. I really want him on my side right now. I'm not sure I'm strong enough to do it alone, regardless of who else will stick by me.

"Isn't that what both of us were doing before all this? You protected your own kind, yes. But you also protected the humans from the rogues, too. Just like me."

"You are asking me to hand my mate over to those that want her dead...or worse." It looks like it's painful for him to say the words, and my chest feels tight. "Maybe a better male could do what you asked, Hel. I'm not that male." His fingers tighten around mine in a punishing grip. "I can't. I will destroy everything and everyone if something happens to you. You must know this."

"Yes, I know. And all that would've been perfect if I couldn't defend myself or I was some unfortunate soul accidentally getting in the middle of this. But I'm not. If I don't try to do something to get one step ahead, they are not going to miraculously go away and forget about me. The jinn will keep coming until they capture me, kill me, or kill everyone I care about. I will not hide and stand back until that happens, Eric. Not for you, not even for myself." Releasing my hold on him, I rub my temples to eleviate my pounding headache. "I don't have a death wish or a desire to play martyr, not anymore. I want to live and not be scared every second of my life that someone will sneak up and stick a knife in my back…or yours, for that matter."

"We can fight them more." He is clenching his fists in rapid succession, as if imagining squeezing the necks of the jinn. "We will get more allies. There are other ways to go about it."

"True, but all of that will take time." Pointing a finger at his chest, I make sure he understands. "Time, we don't have, or we will all get destroyed. The portals are opening all over the world, Eric. We can't be everywhere at once."

"I see there is nothing I can say that will change your mind, cupcake." Warmth spreads through my chest at the nickname I used to hate at the beginning.

"Not on this, monster boy." Smiling sadly at him, my heart breaks, knowing how much it costs him to go along with it. "But I do hope you'll be there to catch me, like always, if I fall."

"I'm definitely planning on catching you, Hel." His eyes blaze, glittering dangerously, and my heart skips a beat.

"What are you doing?" Taking a step back, I watch him warily when his body coils up like a spring.

"Just because I can't stop you from doing insane things doesn't mean I can't do something else." He takes a slow, measured step towards me.

I take another step back.

"Like what, exactly?" Goosebumps cover me from head to toe from the hunger in his eyes. My heart is jackhammering in my chest, and butterflies burst into a frenzy in my lower belly.

"Like reminding you who owns your body and soul, and why you have to make sure you stay alive."

Chapter Twenty-Four

HELENA

My back hits the wall at the same time as Eric's hands press against it on both sides of my head. He is looking down at me and, just from the intensity in his gaze, I can feel the wetness soaking through my pants. Pressing my palms flat on either side of my hips so I don't grab him like I'm starved, because I am, my tongue wets my dry lips. He is watching that like it's the most fascinating thing he has ever seen. I'm already panting from his nearness, my breaths coming out fast in small puffs of air.

Eric's nostrils flare, and I whimper.

How he manages to turn me into a whimpering mess who's ready to beg simply by being near me—even after everything we've already done—is something I don't think I'll ever understand. He smells of male and sin, and I'm spiraling down the rabbit hole so fast my mind is spinning. He wasn't joking when he said he owns my body and soul, because right now, I will offer him my soul on a silver platter, and all he has to do is ask.

Eric presses his chest more firmly to me, my already

hardened nipples rubbing deliciously on the fabric of my shirt. Bumping my head back on the wall, lifting my chin, I close my eyes. I can feel plaster filling up my nails as I dig them in the wall. He is controlling himself just so he can prove his dominance, despite me getting my way in our argument. I know it but damn if I don't want to cave and yank his mouth to mine.

"What do you want, Hel." Eric's deep voice vibrates through my whole body like I'm standing next to a bass speaker in the middle of a concert.

"The same thing you do, monster boy." My voice is breathy and sultry, but I don't look at him. I'm screwed if I do.

He chuckles.

Releasing a shuddering breath, I shift my hips restlessly. I guess he saw that as an invitation. His thick thigh forces its way between my legs, rubbing the seam of my pants over my clit. A low moan wrenches from my chest, and I undulate on his muscled thigh, my body riding his leg with a mind of its own.

"Fuck!" My eyes snap open at his outburst.

His jaw is clenched so tight I can hear his teeth grinding. The arms where he leans the wall to stop himself from crushing me are trembling, the muscles twitching and jumping as I watch. A smile stretches my lips at the way his face is twisted in a snarl because I know how much it costs him to hold back. It costs me too, because I think my fingers will be bleeding from the way I'm clawing at the wall.

"Don't push me, Hel." His words say one thing, but his face tells me another.

He wants to be pushed. And I want to push him.

Keeping my eyes on his, I arch my back, pressing my breasts harder to his chest. His heart is beating as fast as mine. I feel it like a fist thumping on my ribcage. Letting his thigh hold more of my weight, I move against him, giving him a full body rub with each twist. We both moan deep and low at that.

Eric buries his face in my neck, his harsh breaths searing my skin. Tilting my head to the side, I give him more room. He growls like an animal, pulling his lips back over his teeth. I can feel their movement over my skin and the hairs on the back of my neck stand on end. Sniffing, he runs the tip of his nose from my shoulder to the back of my ear and back. Alternating between that and rubbing his face wherever he can, the scrape of his five-o-click shadow on my skin is eliciting sounds from me I'm not aware I'm capable of making.

It occurs to me that I've been recently fighting, running around, bleeding, and I must smell horrible, but it doesn't look like Eric minds. As if reading my mind, he snarls again, lifting his head up and pressing his forehead on mine.

"You smell of blood and sex, Hel. I want to bury myself inside you so deep that you'll never be able to remove me from your body."

Our breaths mingle as we share the air. With every word, his lips graze mine. I can feel the tingling where our skin touches all the way to my core. My channel is clutching emptiness, begging to be filled.

"Do it." I dare him with a sharp look, my belly tightening to extreme levels.

"No." His eyes flash dangerously, and one side of his full lips lift up. "Not until you beg, cupcake."

I'm going to cum just from the look on his face alone. The man is too sinful for his own good, and for mine. But he is not the only one that can tease and bring the other person close to insanity. Still watching him, I shove one hand between us, cupping the thick erection that has been stabbing my hip this whole time. Eric gasps as his hips jerk up, pushing his cock to slide in my palm through his jeans. Tightening my fingers around it, I rub him up and down, in sync with my hips riding his thigh.

"Let's see who begs first." I'm delirious with need, every thought apart from pushing him to a point where he rips our clothes and fills me with his cock is pushed aside.

Eric growls, snarls, and curses more, but his hips continue pumping his cock in my hand, as if he has lost all control. My hips move as well, rubbing my clit on his thigh like we are horny teenagers unable to control our raging hormones. If we don't stop, I know my orgasm is going to knock the breath out of me.

It hits me so suddenly that my eyes roll to the back of my head and stars burst behind my eyelids. Eric crushes his mouth on mine, pushing his tongue past my lips and captures my scream. My body convulses for a long time, Eric moaning viciously in my mouth before I sag, sandwiched between his chest and the wall.

Chapter Twenty-Five

ERIC

My mate knows how to make me crazed with just a blink of her eyes, or a flip of her hair. Her sharp tongue does the same, although I'll never tell her that. If immortals could die from stress or a heart attack, I believe I would've been the first to go.

She is worth it.

Watching her in the throes of her passion is something I will never get tired of. Her cheeks are flushed, her lips swollen from my kisses and her hair wild from the thrashing. I fucking love each and every single thing about this woman. It scares the shit out of me as much as I love it. Her glazed over eyes blink open lazily, and I smile. If she thinks I'm done with her, she has a surprise waiting. I'm not letting her out of this room until she's unable to stand, or walk...

Or both.

She'll eventually figure out what I'm doing, but until then, I'm going to enjoy my mate. I'll stall the inevitable by burying my fears and my cock inside her pliable body, and maybe both of us can disappear in our own world of passion, love, and lust. We won't, but I'll keep trying. The other option is to let her face the jinn, and I'm not ready to think about that yet.

"Eric…" Her voice is raw from her screams, and a prideful smile hurts my cheeks. It's good to know she can resist me as much as I can resist her. In other words, we are both goners.

"Shhh…" Pressing her lips closed with a finger, I rub it over her swollen, red lips. "I'm not done with you, yet."

Her green eyes flash, and she nips at my finger. Nostrils flaring, a groan rumbles in my chest when she closes her teeth over it before sucking it into her warm, wet mouth. My cock strains in my jeans, jerking as if trying to get her attention that she needs to suck on it, not on my finger. Judging by the sultry smile on her face, she knows the effect it has on me. My mate is too pure for the wicked thoughts running through my head right now. Pushing the all-consuming hunger to the back of my mind, I slide my finger out of her mouth.

"We are wearing too many clothes." Placing both palms on my chest, she gives me a nudge. "I missed you, and I need to see all of you."

Stepping back, I wait to see what she does. It takes everything in me not to bend her over and fuck her until none of us can move. But she deserves better, so I wait. Helena pops open the buttons of my jeans, one by one. It's a new torture technique if I've ever seen one. The smile stays on her face, and I narrow my eyes. Maybe she is not as pure as I keep making her out to be. She sure figured out a way to kill me.

Her palm slides inside the jeans, her fingers wrapping around my pulsing cock. My hips jerk at her command, pumping in her hand out of my control. If she keeps it up,

I'm going to spill all over both of us. My hands lift to remove her fingers, but she swats them away. Dropping on her knees, I have no time to even think of stopping her before she swallows my cock down her throat.

"Fuck, Hel!" Snarling and moaning, I tangle my hands in her hair with every intention of pulling her up.

She will have none of that. Moaning and humming, her head keeps bobbing up and down, her tongue swirling wickedly over my length. The harder I pull on her hair so she can release me, the harder she sucks my cock into her mouth. My hips speed up, and my lips curl up as I watch myself fuck her mouth. One of her hands glides off my hard length, and she cups my balls, massaging them between her fingers. Her eyes snap up, locking on mine a second before she sucks hard, the head of my cock hitting the back of her throat, and then she swallows.

"Fuck!" The roar is wrenched out of the depths of my soul. "Fuck, Hel!" Her chuckle sends sparks through my cock, all the way to my toes.

She squeaks when I yank her off my throbbing erection and flip her around. The scrape of her teeth on it only drives me crazy more. Wrapping myself around her like a snake, I jerk her top down, freeing one of her breasts. She laughs, but a deep moan follows when I pinch her nipple between my thumb and forefinger, rolling it between them.

"You wanted a crazy beast." Snarling I nip her ear and hold it between my teeth still talking through a clenched jaw. "You got it."

I shove my other hand down her pants, finding her drenched folds. With no warning, two of my fingers start pumping in her hot channel while I lick, bite, and suck on her neck. Her hips grind on my cock, pushing my sanity further down the abyss.

"Eric." Her head is thrashing left and right, and she keeps moaning. "Fuck me, please. Now, Eric!"

"I thought you'd never ask."

Pulling away just enough to drag her pants down to the middle of her thighs and her top up above her breasts, I sheath myself inside her body with one hard push of my hips. The dagger clatters on the floor. Helena screams, and it only drives my hunger to unbearable levels. Grabbing both her breasts in my hands, I use my hold to pound inside her like a crazed beast. The sound of our skin slapping on skin only adds to my insanity, and I can feel my claws lengthening around her soft flesh.

Panic chokes me, and my thrusting falters for just a beat. The crazy woman wraps her hands over mine, her fingers tangling between my claws as she continues slamming her ass on my groin, impaling herself on my cock. It's the hottest fucking thing I've seen in my entire existence.

"Harder, Eric." She looks over her shoulder at me, and that look on her face is my undoing.

Pulling her flush to my chest, I shove my tongue down her throat, tasting myself on her lips. With one hand, I grab a fistful of her hair, holding her mouth captive, and with the other, I hold her hip so I can pump my hips harder. Her channel is sucking me in like she is as wild and as crazed as I am and doesn't want to let me go. My pumping becomes punishing and brutal, and she matches it, thrust for thrust.

"I'm going to…" Her moaned words end in a scream of my name.

Her tight channel clenches so hard I'm finding it challenging to keep fucking her. She is not letting me slide far enough out so I can move. When I feel it pulsing around my length, sucking it deeper inside her, my entire world falls apart, and my sanity goes with it. The splitting roar that comes out of my mouth shudders the walls around us for as long as I keep pulsing inside her, spilling even my soul through my cock. After what feels like an eternity, I lift my head from her back where I've curled around her, only to see her watching me over her shoulder.

"Well, that was a sure sign that you missed me, too."

My chuckle is embarrassingly weak.

Chapter Twenty-Six

HELENA

After walking out to get a wet cloth so we can clean up, with his jeans unbuttoned and barely hanging on his narrow hips —you know, who cares about modesty around here—Eric holds onto me as if I'll try and escape. I say nothing because I'm holding onto him the same way. Okay, fine, I'm stalling. I'm sure the entire neighborhood heard us having sex, and I'm not in a rush to see the others. Groaning, I press my face closer to Eric's neck.

"What's up, cupcake?" Eric is trying to act like he doesn't know why I dread leaving this room.

I know that he knows why.

Apparently, there is a cot here, and that's where we are curled up around each other at the moment. I didn't notice it when we first walked in. No one can blame me for not seeing anything when Eric is around. The man sucks the attention out of everything within a mile radius around him. I might be biased, but there is also no denying the guy is hot as hell.

I snort.

"What's going on inside your head, Hel?" He kisses the top of my head, a habit he developed that I really like, and rubs his cheek over my hair.

"I was just thinking that you're hot as hell." A surprised chuckle coming from him bounces my head on his chest. "Yes, I know. I'm brilliant like that, coming up with puns and all."

"I see." His voice sounds amused, but also, I can hear the satisfaction in it.

"We do need to leave this room, as much as I don't want to." Pressing my chin on his chest, I look into his eyes. His arms tighten momentarily. "I wanna see if Maddison found out something from your groupie and we need to start coming up with a plan on how to do this."

My joke, calling Lauren his groupie, falls flat.

"I still don't like it." His gaze darkens.

"Neither do I, but we do what we gotta do." Shrugging, I peck his lips.

Eric lets me lift up and sit next to him reluctantly. I'm moving around him now like he is a dangerous snake and I don't want to startle it. I have a feeling if I make one wrong move, he will lock me up in one of the rooms to stop me from moving on with my plan.

I seriously wouldn't put it past him to do something like that.

"Promise me something, Hel." He laces his fingers through mine.

"If I can, no problem." I guess that was not the right thing to say because a muscle jumps in his jaw. I watch him evenly.

"Promise me that if anything feels strange, no matter how insignificant it seems..." His Adam's apple bobs up and down. "You'll get the fuck out of there."

"That's easy." Smiling, I bring his fingers to my lips, giving them a kiss. "I was honest that I have no death wish. I'll be out of there so fast their heads will be spinning."

"And you will not leave this realm under any circumstance." His eyes narrow.

I roll mine so hard at that, I can see the inside of my skull. "I might be reckless, Eric, but I'm not an idiot."

His lips twitch, and he frowns at that like he is upset with himself for wanting to smile. I'm funny, damn it. He should've laughed. So, I poke him in the ribs. His legs jack-knife on the cot and he jumps up, holding both palms facing me to keep me away.

A wicked grin blooms on my face.

"How interesting." I stand up slowly, while he takes steps back, eyeing me warily. "I never pegged you for being ticklish."

"Helena, stand back." His face is so serious I can't help but burst out laughing.

"Umm…" Tapping my lips after I'm done laughing my ass off, I pretend I'm considering it. "I think not."

Springing on him, I keep poking him anywhere I can reach. It's a good thing Eric is trying not to hurt me while fending off my deadly fingers. He is cursing up a storm, laughing and growling, even snapping his teeth at me a few times and making me scream. The weight that was pressing on my chest ever since he was hurt lightens more, and the longer I listen to his deep laughter, the easier it is to breathe.

Eric is usually serious. He has that trademark smirk that is permanently keeping one corner of his full lips quirked up, yes. But he very rarely laughs or has any fun just for the sake of it. Pretty much the same as me. So, it feels wonderful to have this moment we share, even if I would've preferred for it not to be in this building. His face is open, the line between his eyebrows smoothed out, and he looks much younger. If you don't know he is centuries old, you'll think we are the same age. Maybe him being a year or two older.

"You okay, Hel?"

I didn't notice I stopped poking him and I'm just sitting here, straddling his chest and staring, while he is sprawled on his back on the floor. Smiling, I push the hair off his forehead, tracing his firm jaw, high cheekbones, nose, and eyebrows with my fingers. When I touch his lips, he kisses the pads of my fingers, and my heart gets too large for my chest.

"I've never been better." His eyebrow goes up, and I laugh. "This right here is why I have to do this. I want us to have more times like this, Eric. When we don't fight or run for our lives. Or have to go to Hell to close portals and other bullshit." I press my fingers harder on his lips to keep him quiet. "I know nothing can change who or what I am. I'll never be completely safe and left alone. But I'm sure we can find a way to avoid most of the other problems if we get rid of the jinn. I feel it in my bones that I'm right."

He kisses my fingers one more time before removing my hand from his face gently. "You don't have to keep convincing me; I know that nothing I say can change your mind. I'll go along with this insanity of yours, and for all our sakes I hope it works out well." I push off the floor, tugging him up with me while he speaks. "Because if it doesn't…I'm not sure what I'm capable of doing."

"I know." Wrapping my arms around his waist, I hug him close. "Everything will work out, though. I know it will."

I wish things are ever as easy as that.

Chapter Twenty-Seven

HELENA

Eric tugs me along with him through the hallways. I'm avoiding everyone's eyes as they pass by us, but my face is on fire. Maybe none of them care. For all I know, they were not even here to hear my screams, but I can't help it. Not because I'm a prude or anything. It's just that whenever Eric and I are intimate, I see it as something personal, something that I want to keep only between the two of us. My inability to keep myself from screaming at the top of my lungs notwithstanding.

Monster boy, on the other hand, struts around with his chest puffed up so much you'd think they just named him the king of Heaven and Hell. He even grins at me every time he catches my eye, like he is expecting me to give him applause for an excellent performance. The performance was more than excellent, if my still-trembling legs have anything to say about it, but he can keep on dreaming if he's waiting on me to acknowledge that in public.

Hell to the no.

Thankfully, we reach the room where we left the rest of

our group. Eric stops at the closed door, giving me a raised eyebrow. Blowing out a deep breath, I release his hand, wiping my sweaty palms off my pants. Steeling my spine and widening my stance, I press my lips firmly and nod at him. I watch his hand as it wraps around the knob, loosening my arms at my sides. With a sharp twist of his wrist, he swings it open.

A flurry of movement strikes through the space, slamming at my legs, and I snitch a handful of blond curls. The Trowe is vibrating while clutching at my leg, and Eric roars with laughter. We learned the little bugger's trick, so I was prepared for him this time instead of kicking him like a ball.

"Mistress…" Narsi hisses in long, creepy intervals, and everyone joins Eric's laughter.

"Hello, Narsi." Still holding a fistful of his hair so he can't climb me like a tree, I shuffle awkwardly in the room. "You haven't seen me in an hour, if that. A very long time, right?"

"Yessss." He looks absolutely thrilled that I've acknowledged my absence.

Shaking my head, I ignore Colt especially, because I can see he is barely holding himself together so he doesn't make a smartass remark. My glare only makes him grin more, and I'm grateful when Beelzebub punches him in the gut. The pained groan and the loud whoosh of air exiting Colt's lungs is a piece of music to my ears. Nodding at the fallen, I smile when his red eyes sparkle with humor.

"It serves you right," I tell Eric's twin, lifting my nose up.

Even Raphael roars in laughter from that.

"I see I missed all the fun." Right on our heels, Maddison walks in, and all fun in the room gets sucked out.

Not because of her, obviously, but because of the dark

cloud of doom hanging over our heads. Eric sits next to me, Narsi wiggling his tiny butt between us until he gets comfortable. He still has his fingers twisted in my pants, probably in case I decide to run away from him. I can see now the Trowe is going to be a problem in executing my plan. But, first thing first.

"Did she tell you anything useful?" Eric beats me to it.

"She did, yes." Maddison is still holding herself as usual, but since I stare at her too much when she's around, I can notice the guardedness in her eyes.

"How did you manage that?" Colt looks her up and down as if seeing someone that looks like she doesn't want to break a nail by lifting a finger.

I kick his foot that's outstretched in my direction.

"I had help." The grin she gives him sends a shiver down my spine.

I notice the specks of blood she has forgotten to wipe out, or hasn't seen it maybe, on her neck and one side of her jaw. Maddison wouldn't leave a crumb on her, little less a smear of blood. I forgot all that I was going to say about that when I follow the direction of her finger. Leviathan walks right behind her with a scowl on his face. I guess I missed him not being present thanks to the Trowe. Maybe someone should tell the dragon that he will look better if he stops glaring like that all the time, but it'll be useless because even with his face scrunched up like that, he is too good looking by human standards. His icy blue eyes snap to mine, and I keep my mouth shut.

"What do we know?" Eric frowns at Leviathan until dragon boy looks away.

They are going to kill me if they all keep acting like two-year-olds.

"They are operating from a warehouse not far from

here, in this realm." Leaning a shoulder on the wall, her arms fold over her chest. "Quite smart if you ask me. None of us would think to start checking warehouses looking for jinn like they are rats."

"I don't think the jinn are expecting any of us to look for them, period." Narsi hisses like an angry cat, so I pet his head to shut him up. "The one me, Beelzebub, and Colt fought was very cocky. He acted like an elephant staring at an ant while he was talking. I know he was sure in his head that there is nothing we can do if he decides to kill us."

Exchanging a look with both Colt and Beelzebub, I don't let my eyes linger too long on them. We told Eric that we fought the jinn, we just skipped some details. Like splitting up, or like the jinn almost killing me. Okay, we skipped telling him all of it apart from we fought the jinn and we won. If he knows everything, there is no way a piece of my hair can exit this building for about a hundred years or so.

"She said there is one jinn that's in charge of the rest of them in that warehouse," Maddison says, but she is too perceptive for my own good. She noticed the looks we exchanged, and I hope she doesn't say anything. "And that Mammon spends most of his time in this realm there."

"We should go scout the place first." Everyone perks up at that, including Narsi. "I just wanna know if that one jinn that Lauren told you about is the one that looks like me, or we are dealing with a lackey."

"If we get lucky"—Beelzebub claps his plate-sized hands, making me jump before he rubs them gleefully—"we might get our hands on that fucker Mammon. I want to show him why he needs hordes of demons between us so he can fight me."

Colt and Leviathan get vocal at that, I guess it's a sore spot that Mammon got us all bloodied before we got our butts out of Hell. Eric joins in their enthusiasm, too. I watch Raphael from the corner of my eye, and my chest warms up when I see him nodding and getting involved with everyone else. I can't imagine it being easy on him that he is all alone, one of his kind in the middle of us here. His yellow eyes turn on me, and he smiles like he knows what I'm thinking.

"This is my fight too, Helena. We are all in this together, and I see no one here as below me just because I come from Heaven. They are trying to destroy all of us, and I'm sure many of my brothers and sisters would join given a chance. They just don't know who to trust right now, and I cannot blame them. Heaven was in flames when I escaped with my life." My eyes burn with unshed tears at the sadness on Raphael's face as he hangs his head.

The new shock of the century comes when Eric grabs Raphael's shoulder, squeezing reassuringly. "We will get the fuckers. We will clean them all out of Heaven and Hell."

None of us believe it'll be that easy, but it's nice to hear it. I smile gratefully at Eric.

"What are we waiting for then?" Pushing off the floor, I almost fall back on my ass because Narsi is still playing a koala on my leg. "Let's go see what we are dealing with."

Chapter Twenty-Eight

HELENA

We have to split up in groups because Maddison apparently has an army of demons at her beck and call that none of us knew anything about. Eric knew about them, but he didn't think she still had them around, considering the situation. He was wrong. Staring with my mouth open, I watched the groups of ten to twelve huge horned demons disappear in the darkness. We had to wait for a few hours before leaving the safe house for the night to fully cover Atlanta, and the time is finally here.

It's really odd not to feel the repulsion that would typically pass through me when looking at demons. I watch them blend in with the night, finding myself hoping they are safe and don't get killed. I'm not sure if it's because I know Eric's true form now, or because after spending time in Hell and seeing myself in another person numbed me to everything else. It's funny how perspectives change.

Stranger than that is seeing George and Cass watching the whole thing without blinking an eye. They are hunters like me, yes, but neither of them has demon blood in their veins. Yet, I see them nodding at some of the demons like they are friends. I guess it's true when we say the enemy of my enemy is my friend. But no one here is my adversary. Not unless they try to hurt humans in any case. Even now, I'll have no problem introducing them to my dagger.

When the last group of demons disappears, George and Cass join Colt, Raphael, and Beelzebub, and all of them take off down the street at a jog. Eric takes my hand, and we follow swiftly with Maddison, Leviathan, and Narsi on our heels. I hope the Trowe keeps quiet or we might get in a ton of shit. Reaching at my back, I assure myself my dagger is there. We don't plan on fighting tonight, but you never know. All sorts of creatures are walking the streets of Atlanta now.

"Three blocks down and head to your right. The warehouse is all the way at the end of the boulevard, facing a hill," Maddison whispers softly before she and Leviathan whir off from us and are gone.

"I should've fucking known," Eric grumbles as we speed up. "It slipped my mind."

"Known what?" Breathing through my nose, I try to keep my heart rate steady.

"I know the place we are going." He releases my hand so he can clench his fists, and Narsi snatches it like a spider monkey. "I was watching the place the night I found you in that damn building." Another growl is followed by a couple of curses. "Maddison was with me that night...well, the damn jinn impersonating her."

"Now that we know the jinn don't want me dead, I think that bomb going off was meant either for you or Raphael." I think I'm going to puke just thinking about it. They almost killed Raphael.

"Yeah, well, too bad for the fuckers both of us are

alive." Eric puts a burst of speed in his anger, and I follow him, huffing and puffing like a freight train.

Damn it, aren't I an abomination? Shouldn't it come with the same perks too?

Turning down the boulevard Maddison told us about, I can already feel that things are not as they should be. My internal GPS goes haywire, alarms blaring in my head. Even Narsi whimpers, but I'm starting to think that he does that when he is reacting to my distress, or any strong emotion. Tugging him so he moves faster, I keep running. Eric has already put some distance between us, and I will hate to be the last person to get there. Especially with all my bravado on infiltrating the jinn.

We are almost there when all hell breaks loose.

Demons similar to the ones we fought in Hell come out from everywhere. If I didn't know better, I'd say they were waiting for us. But that would mean we have a jinn in our close group and I'm sure that we don't. Or I could be wrong since they did trick us a few times and not just once. Narsi yanks on my hand hard, bending me down just in time for my head to avoid the large boot aimed at it.

"Thanks, Narsi." With a round kick, I send the demon flying into a few of them behind him. "You are a number one sidekick."

I feel Eric's back on mine when he materializes next to me. Sliding the dagger out, I ignore the screams and crunching sound coming from where I know Narsi is. I don't even look because one, I can hear him hissing like he's deranged, and two, because I know he is probably eating some of them. My stomach lurches at the thought.

"They were spread out to protect the warehouse." Eric grunts, his back bumping on mine as he punches and kicks. "We didn't think ahead, as usual."

"I thought"—Slashing with the dagger, I use one of the demon's arms as a hold to kick two others in their snarling faces. I stab him in the eye when my feet touch the ground —"that you like traps. If I remember correctly, Maddison said you specifically look for them."

Eric chuckles at that. "That was when I didn't have a mate with a target on her forehead."

"Thanks, monster boy." Wincing when a claw digs into my arm, I bite my lip so I don't make a sound and distract Eric. "I appreciate the reminder."

"You are hurt." Snapping, Eric turns into a whirlwind.

I stumble when his wings burst out and his body grows larger. All my movements stop because everywhere I turn, all I can see is Eric's back and his wings. He is moving around me so fast that if I try and fight, I'll probably stab him accidentally. So, I stand like an idiot for extended moments until he finally stops in front of me. His chest is heaving, and his head is hanging down as he collects himself. Slowly he goes back to his human form, the beautiful wings disappearing into his back.

My eyes widen when I look at the street, and all I see is bodies piled up on top of one another. Like a low wall, they surround us on all sides. Eric blows out a breath while I turn in a small circle, looking at what he did. He wasn't joking when he said he will go insane if I get hurt. My eyebrows have climbed all the way to my hairline from the sight around me. And then, my gaze lands on Narsi who is licking his lips while blood is dripping down his chin.

"I ate his face..." The Trowe hisses happily, making Eric snort.

Groaning, I cover my face with my hand.

Chapter Twenty-Nine

HELENA

"Let's get out of the open." Eric grabs my hand, pulling me along with him in the shadows of the scarce houses on the street.

"I hope the others didn't get into too much trouble." Hanging onto him like he is my lifeline, I find it difficult to swallow past my dry mouth.

"They're fine." Glancing over his shoulder, to assure himself that I'm not ready to kneel over I'm sure, Eric keeps moving. "These were not high-level demons. They shouldn't have been that strong at any rate. The jinn are feeding them power and making them stronger."

Ignoring Narsi because his bloodied face and creepy smile are etched on my retinas, I dart my eyes left and right, expecting more to spring at us at any moment. I told everyone we should act unpredictably to get one step ahead of the jinn, but if this tells me anything, I think we did exactly what they expected us to do. God damn it! Eric's comment finally penetrates my swirling thoughts.

"Wait." My stomach drops to my toes. "They can do

that? Like, make others more powerful? I thought they can only change their powers for themselves when they steal someone's identity."

"They can do it temporarily, from what I've heard." Eric doesn't sound worried at all about this, which doesn't surprise me.

"We were ambushed," Maddison speaks from right behind me.

With my heart jumping in my throat, I release Eric's hold, whirling around and slashing in a wide arch in her direction. The dagger flares, bursting in gold and red light as I watch it horrified, slicing the air right at Maddison's neck. The slight widening of her eyes is the only indication that she realized her error and shouldn't have scared me. I can't stop my reaction, although I do try to jerk my hand back before it connects to her skin.

My jaw unhinges itself, dropping to my chest when the beautiful woman in front of me bends her upper body backward, following the blade in its descent, the sharp edge missing her throat by a hair. It's like she's breaking the physics of time and space, her body looking boneless for a second, her long, red mane spreading around her head like living flames. The strength of my attack would've taken me down if a hand didn't grab my arm, holding me upright.

Maddison straightens, smoothing her hair with one hand.

"No sneaking up," she says nonchalantly like I wasn't about to open her throat like a zipper pouch. "Understood."

Snickering, Eric pulls away so he can make room for Maddison and Leviathan to hunker next to us. I'm still gaping, part in horror, part in awe at what happened. The tightening of the fingers still gripping my forearm snap me out of it and I see that it was Leviathan that tried to stop me from stabbing at Maddison. His eyes are eerily glowing on his handsome face, the look in them warning me not to touch him. The fallen is struggling for control, and I go unnaturally still, the danger I find myself in freezing me in place.

"Umm, guys!" Doing my best not to startle him, I keep my gaze locked on his, "Little help here." I really don't want to hurt him, but I feel that power that destroyed the jinn surge up through my chest, ready to be unleashed.

"Stand down, Leviathan." Maddison sounds exasperated, and without a care grabs his arm, yanking him away. "I was at fault."

Eric is looming over my shoulder, heat coming off him in waves. I can feel his rage like a caress on my skin, the damn power inside me eating it up like I am starved for it. Panic seizes my lungs at that, but Leviathan blinks, his face clearing out. Shaking his head, the fallen frowns and looks at all of us like it's our fault he almost went nuts. Well, it's my fault, but I didn't ask them to scare me. I'm little jumpy right now, so sue me.

Just like that, the air settles like nothing happened and I take a deep breath. If we keep it up like this, we might kill each other by the time we must deal with the jinn. Eric wraps me up in his arms, angling his body so that he stands between Leviathan and me, and I don't push him away. Snuggling closer to his chest, I breathe him in.

Maddison leans in, looking down the street.

When I glance down, because it's a little too quiet for my liking, to check on my sidekick, I see Narsi crouched on all fours, his ugly, wrinkled face tilted like a bird at Leviathan. Bile rises in my throat and, reaching out, I snatch a handful of his hair, pulling him to me.

"No more eating faces, Narsi!" Whisper-yelling at him, I drag the Trowe on the other side of me.

He looks like he is pouting, but I'm so unnerved by the whole face-eating thing that I push it to the back of my mind with the rest of the stuff that I'm going to freak about later. It's very fortunate that we get moving again as well. Staying alive trumps creepy sidekicks any day of the week.

We all move silently through the night in a direction that Maddison is taking us. Leviathan is glued to her, ignoring the rest of us, which is fine by me. Now that I think about it, the dragon guy acts weird around Maddison. He either likes her or hates her. You can never tell these things since he always looks like he is about to punch you in the throat.

"I see Colt." Maddison glances at us and bolts down the street, skipping the hiding part.

When I see the group of demons, double the size of what Eric and I dealt with, surrounding our friends, I run after her with everything in me. Narsi releases an excited hiss, and I tune him out so I don't puke.

We barrel through the demons as soon as we reach them. Maddison is stealthy, twirling around and picking them off one by one from the back. Narsi disappears excitedly through the crowd gathered in front of us. I guess it's a good meal day for the Trowe, I hope he doesn't get heartburn if he eats too much. A burst of hysterical laughter comes out from me at that disturbing thought.

Eric moves with his usual grace, every punch and kick flowing gracefully like a macabre dance. I slash and hit everything I can get my hands on, the warm blood spraying around us, saturating the air with the coppery scent. Leviathan is the only one not fighting. He simply charges the demons from their back, sending them flying all over the place like bowling pins.

When we reach our friends, we all form a circle and start making quick work of whatever is left of the demons. The nagging at the back of my mind gets stronger, and I manage to look around. My chest contracts in a metal vice when I see what's been bothering me.

"Where is Raphael?" My heart is beating in my throat.

"We lost him a block away." Colt grunts. "They trapped us between buildings, and we had to split up."

"Calm down, Helena," Beelzebub shouts, ripping the horns from a demon and throwing them like a boomerang at those closest to him. "He will be fine. It's not like the jinn are trying to capture him."

His words stop me in my tracks, and I almost end up impaled on a sword. Colt kicks the blade away from my chest, staring at me like I've lost my mind. And maybe I have. My brain hurts from thoughts fighting for attention as I stand like a statue in the middle of a life and death fight. Colt is joined by Eric and Beelzebub, the three of them surrounding me with their bodies so I don't get killed, because right now I can't fight. I can't even move from the crippling realization that followed the seemingly insignificant comment on Beelzebub's part.

"We must find Raphael!" I tell no one in particular. I'm not even sure they heard me.

"The feathered fucker is the least of our worries," Colt snaps, obviously hearing my words. "He can and will take care of himself."

The twins are deaf when it's something they don't want to hear. I love Eric to death, but he will ignore everything I say because he thinks he is protecting me. There is no way I can get out from between Colt and Eric on my own, so I latch onto Beelzebub's arm, squeezing with all my might to get his attention.

"They have my father, Lucifer, and Mammon is willingly helping them." Beelzebub looks at me like I'm insane, but I push through, urgency ringing clear in my voice. "They also have my mother and Michael, Beelzebub. Number three is important from what I know. They are missing an Archangel. Tonight wasn't about me at all. They set a trap to get to Raphael."

"Fuck!" Beelzebub roars, and everyone, including the rest of our group, jolts back from him. "Fuck!" His wings burst out and, scooping me up, he flings us in the air.

My scream is joined by Eric's pissed off roar. Shit!

Chapter Thirty

RAPHAEL

I should know that they'll set up traps in case someone discovers their nest in this world. We have battled many times through the ages, and yet I still keep forgetting to think things through before I jump in with everyone else. I could've seen this coming, and my slight might cost Helena her life.

"Fool!" Chastising myself under my breath, I fight off the few demons that follow me in this stinking alley.

There were more of them gunning for me when I had to split up from the others. Like a swarm of insects, they kept coming, and it was either merge away from the others to give us a fighting chance, or all of us perish this night. I am so tired lately that the idea of eternal sleep is not as worrisome as it would've been a few centuries ago. Keeping Helena safe, the promise I made that fateful day, is the only thing keeping me fighting.

Snorting, I kick off the pest trying to get his claws on me. The stinging of many cuts and raked skin from claws gives me the alertness I usually would've been lacking. I'm a healer, so I do not relish a fight. I'm a warrior as well, so I will give them what they want.

Because you gave your word, my mind reminds me, as if I'll ever be able to forget biding myself to that oath.

There are fewer demons now, and a frown pulls my eyebrows over my eyes when I don't see many bodies littering the trash-laden ground. The puddles of murky water mix with the spilled demon blood, stinking up the enclosed ally with the scent of death. Where did they go? I hope not after the others, because all of them are needed to keep the girl safe.

"Nowhere for you to run angel." A demon gets closer, his sharp teeth bared in a warning. "They said you should live, but not that you be unharmed."

His grin grows at my confusion, but I learned a long time ago not to trust a word that comes out of their mouth. Kicking out, my boot connects with his gut, sending him crashing to the opposite wall. My blood rushes through my body, the adrenaline exciting me for the fight. I push it down. I have to fight, but I don't have to like it.

"I will make you bleed all your holy grace before you beg to be killed." The demon lifts himself up, glaring at me.

"Or you'll put me to sleep with your sweet words, demon." I don't have to fake the tiredness in my words. I do it for Helena, but I will not do it for the scum. "Shall we fight, or shall we sit down to chat?"

"There will be plenty of time for chatting, don't you worry, Raphael." His face contorts with hatred, and he throws himself at me.

His words make no sense, so I ignore them. More of them spill in through the mouth of the alley, blocking the way out. Not that I was trying to escape. The longer I keep them occupied here, the fewer there will be to go after

Helena. That is the reason I tell myself, and not the fact that every cut and bruise they inflict is a punishment I give myself.

I sink into a trance-like state, my body moving in a well-practiced form of twists and turns, kicks and flips. Block, turn, punch, flip, kick, repeat. They keep coming, after what feels like hours, even two or three at a time. My skin is burning everywhere their claws or weapons touch, but I don't stop. Either they will stop, or I will tire. For now, we keep our dance moving in a whirlwind of limbs and bodies.

Shouts different from the constant sound I've been hearing pull me out of the state I'm in. My eyes widen when the horde blocking the alley thins, demons dropping left and right. The air freezes my lungs when Helena barrels through them, stopping at my side. I can't tell what kind of expression is on my face, but it must be comical because she grins at me.

"Need help?" Her knees bend as she readies herself to fight.

All I can do is blink at her.

I made an oath to protect her. Yet, here she is, running head-first in the fray to help me. I've always been a loner, keeping to myself and watching everyone from the corner I built for myself. So, they left me to my own devices, not getting involved in my life. But not her, no. She doesn't even ask if you want her help. She barges in, no excuses or apologies.

So much like her mother.

"Stop gaping and let's get out of here." She attacks the remaining demons with relish.

"You shouldn't have come, Helena." Snapping out of the musings, I join her. "I was keeping them away. Everything was under control."

She gives me a look saying I'm full of crap and I can't help but smile. The upturn of my lips falters when I see her punching and kicking at the demons. Frowning, I try to look around while still doing my own part in getting us out of here.

"You lost your dagger?" I hiss when a demon gives me a nasty gash on my ribs.

"Yeah, I dropped it. We can get it on our way back." She already reached the mouth of the alley. "Come on, let's get out of here."

Taking the hand she offers, I let her lead me away. Like silk, her hair is streaming behind her while we dash through the twisted back streets of this neighborhood. It's strange that she holds my hand, and I hope Eric will not get all territorial if he sees it, but I can't let go because she has a very firm grip on me. I'm debating on sending healing through her arm, although she doesn't look hurt at all. I decide to ask her when we find the others. I'm not at the top of my strength right now anyway.

"Why are you alone? What happened? Are any of them hurt?" I know it was stupid to leave them. She could've been taken for my stupidity.

"We had to split up to look for you." She looks over her shoulder at me. "You scared the shit out of me."

"I can take care of myself, but you have my gratitude." Smiling, I almost topple over her when she stops.

"Let's take a breath here." She pulls me between two small buildings, and I have no idea where we are. "All this running got me tired." She holds her hand on her side, and guilt eats a hole in my chest.

"Let me see, Helena." Pulling her hand away, I look her over for some injury I might've missed. "I will heal you."

My whole body turns to granite when her small hand cups my face.

"You are always so kind, Raphael." Looking at me through her lashes, her thumb rubs my jaw gently. "Always ready to take care of me."

"I said I'd protect you, Helena." Expanding my chest, I push out the air through my nose harshly. "My word is my vow."

"I don't know how I didn't see it until now." Her voice sounds hesitant, making me frown.

"What do you mean?"

"You are always there, ready to heal me, protect me. I'm an idiot for thinking it's just what you do." Her cheeks redden, and my chest feels tight. "When I couldn't find you, I thought I was going to die, Raphael. That's when I understood how much I care about you."

My mouth is dry and hanging open, and my eyebrows hide in my hairline. I'm staring stupefied at the woman in front of me like I've never seen her before. At least she doesn't laugh or call me an idiot, thank goodness.

"I know that you love me, Raphael." She smiles. "I see it now, and I feel the same. Eric was a mistake, a demon trick, or even the jinn playing their games. I don't want to go back there, please."

"Helena." I sound like I'm about to faint as if I'm human. All the air leaves my lungs in a rush. "I swore to protect you, Helena. And I do love you...just not like you think." My throat closes in hopes it'll stop the words that want to come out. "I...I love your mother, Helena. I swore to her that I'd protect you."

"How unfortunate. You couldn't make this easy, could you?" Her face distorts in an ugly mask, and before I realize what's happening, fire in my chest folds me over. "The

154

stupid bitch can't even seduce a fucking angel. Satan's daughter, my ass."

"Helena…" Dropping on my knees, I watch her wide-eyed.

"Helena is a little busy right now, angel." The creature smirks at me, and the world turns dark.

Chapter Thirty-One

HELENA

"We left him around here," Beelzebub growls while I twist in his arms, looking for Raphael. "Stop moving or I'll drop you."

"I don't care where you left him." Snapping at him, I dig my nails in his skin. "Fly faster, damn it!"

"There!" His jaw clenches and the wings fold close to his body.

So I don't scream, I bite my lip and taste blood when we arrow down at the group of demons. They are not fighting, just standing around as if confused, and dread overrides my panic at the reckless flying. The idiots may all have wings and are used to this shit, but I'm not a freaking bird. I freak out every time I'm in the air because I was meant to have solid ground under my feet.

Beelzebub drops on his feet, my teeth rattling from the hard impact of his landing. Two seconds later, a pissed off Eric drops next to us, snatching me like a toy out of Beelzebub's arms. I glare at him, but he glares back, so I keep my snarky comments to myself because I don't have time to argue right now. Plus, Beelzebub is already making quick work of the confused demons. By the time we grapple so I can untangle myself from Eric's arms, which are sticking to me like Velcro even after I remove them, only one demon is left dangling in Beelzebub's grip.

"Where is the Archangel?" The fallen sounds so pissed that I want to tell him where Raphael is, although I have no damn clue.

"You are too late." The stupid demon gloats, and his eyes bulge out when the hand around his throat tightens.

"Let's try again," Beelzebub snarls. "Remember when I send you back to Hell, I will follow shortly to keep you company there. No jinn will help you while I learn to knit with your guts."

I walk up behind the demon and press my dagger on his bare back. The searing of skin and the stench of burnt skin makes me wrinkle my nose. The beast screams so loud, my ears are ringing.

"Or, I can end him for good, if he likes," I tell Beelzebub, and he grins proudly at me.

"The jinn lead him away." The demon whimpers.

"Which jinn?" Nausea makes me lightheaded because I know what he is going to say.

"The one that looks like you." Pulling my hand back, I'm about to stab him, but Beelzebub drops him in a heap.

"Let's go." The fallen storms off, his face turned up as he sniffs the air like a hunting dog.

I was going to ask if we should kill the demon, but a ball of energy tackles the curled-up asshole, rolling along with it a few feet. Narsi pops his head out, grinning like a fool. How he got here so fast is beyond me.

"I will eat his face..." The Trowe hisses before opening his jaw unnaturally wide.

I turn my back fast, swallowing the bile.

"Oh my God..." I think I'm going to faint. "What's with the damn Trowe and face eating?"

"We need to find Raphael." Eric knows how to snap me out of it and, thanks to my gruesome sidekick, his glare is gone, replaced by a barely-contained smile. "That's what a Haltija does when they are protecting someone..."

"I don't wanna hear it." Lifting a hand up, I stop whatever else he was going to say. "Let's just go and find the Archangel."

Beelzebub is already disappearing around a corner, and I hurry after him, unable to stifle the munching sounds from behind me. Revulsion sends a shudder through me, and I shake like a dog with fleas. Eric chuckles but wisely keeps his mouth shut. After a few twists and turns, I almost jump out of my skin when Colt shows up out of nowhere. He just falls in step with us like he was always there. His smirk tells me he knows that he spooked me.

I lose sight of Beelzebub for just a second, and his roar curdles the blood in my veins. I bolt for him, but the twins are faster. Thankfully, they each grab an arm, tugging me along with them, my boots barely scraping the ground. When we reach the tight space between two buildings, panic chokes me.

The jinn that looks like me is standing in a wide stance over Raphael's limp body. There is something like a shard sticking out from the center of the Archangel's chest, and his blood is soaking down his shirt. Beelzebub is on his knees, clawing at his throat, ripping the skin with his nails. I freeze when I come face to face with myself, that strange, stupefied state overtaking my thought process entirely. Until Eric and Colt drop to their knees, their mouths open in a silent scream.

Something in me flips.

It's nothing drastic or too powerful to handle. It's very subtle, fluttering like a butterfly's wings in my chest. One second, I'm panicking, the next a calm washes over me like spring rain. My entire focus centers on the jinn, the edges of my periphery dimming into shadows.

Our gazes lock.

A smirk starts lifting her mouth a little too soon. She thinks she has won. That she has Raphael and I can do nothing but watch her take him. My mate and the other two men that have fought by my side are unable to breathe, and this bitch thinks I will tuck my tail and run. Obviously, she doesn't know me well enough to know I have a knee-jerk reaction to shit like this when I'm cornered.

My anger surges through me like lava. The ground under our feet shakes so violently the jinn flies to the wall, her head cracking like an egg on the bricks. Like in a dream, I stand still while the world around me shatters. The golden glow that destroyed a horde of demons in Hell flows through my hands, wrapping around the four men in this tight space. The buildings on both sides start falling apart, large chunks embedding themselves deep into the earth. The concrete rises like hills around us, thankfully not on top of the men.

The jinn shakes itself up, rising as well, with fury in its eyes. The image it has taken flickers like a dying lightbulb before the too-perfect creature is staring at me from across the space. In the back of my mind, I'm aware that I should be dead just by seeing it with my mortal eyes.

But I'm not.

I'm neither dead nor mortal. And this evil being that cares about nothing but itself thinks I will stand back while it devastates everything I care about, everything I've known.

A matching smirk pulls my lips at the confusion on the jinn's face. It seems they don't know everything there is to know about the abomination that is Helena. And this jinn will not live long enough to warn the others.

Acceptance stares at me from the too-perfect face of the jinn. Death stares back at it through mine.

Then, we clash.

Chapter Thirty-Two

HELENA

When our bodies collide, a sonic boom blasts everything away from us, leaving a clear area an entire block wide. A quick prayer floats through my head that the men are not hurt, or worse, from the strength of it. I shouldn't have worried because the golden glow surrounding them keeps them cocooned like eggs in the crater-like nest.

The jinn fights with desperation, wild and brutal. Every hit I take, I feel the bones breaking, shattering from the force of the impact. And I feel the excruciating pain of them molding back together, healing faster than they are being broken. It all blends in, feeding me with a constant euphoria of such strong emotions, my skin feels like it'll split open, unable to contain it.

We keep exchanging punches and kicks, swirling around each other like possessed. The jinn looks reckless, but I notice it stays away from my dagger the best it can. Its foot slams me in the center of my chest, caving my ribcage like paper and sending me flying a yard away. When I drop on my knees, a horrible scream is ripped from my soul while my bones put themselves together. Through the tears streaming down my face, I see the three men clawing at the golden glow holding them prisoner. They will not escape until either one of us dies.

Hanging my chin to my chest, I stay on my knees, panting. My entire body is shivering and shaking. The breath is freezing cold when it passes through my lungs, which are burning up from the inferno building inside of me. Blood drips down my fingers, soaking the ground, and my hair sticks to my face. I feel the jinn when it stops in front of me, its gloating like a tangible thing in the air.

"You can't win." The voice that speaks is alluring, sweet, and tempting like poison before it takes your life away.

I feel the teardrop gathering at the tip of my nose, growing larger and heavier before it falls and splatters on the ground, disappearing like it never existed. Just like my heart is breaking, the cracks open wide at all the injustice around me. Power rules over love or compassion, in this realm or the next. And we all pay the price of having a soft heart.

My knees tremble when I stagger and wobble around, lifting up on my feet. The jinn laughs, and it breaks the last of my sanity. The soft chuckle grows in volume, and the jinn takes a wary step back. Slowly, I lift my head up, gazing at its face with crazed eyes. My laughter echoes around us until it abruptly stops.

"I never fight to win." Faster than lightning, I bury my dagger in its chest. "I fight to survive."

I hold the jinn to me like we are lovers about to share a kiss. I don't look away from its eyes until the light in them dims and the life fueling it disappears. I don't release the body until it disappears in my arms like it never existed.

Only after that, I drop on the ground, the golden light around me winking out.

"Hel!" Eric is next to me in a split second, gathering me in his arms.

"Help, Raphael." Cupping his face, I smile when he nuzzles my palm.

"Colt removed the crystal from his chest." Pushing the hair from my face, his deep, green eyes look panicked. "Hopefully he will heal on his own."

"What?" Frowning, I try to push him away. "What do you mean he will heal on his own. They healed him before."

Eric releases his hold on me reluctantly, and I stumble to the Archangel. I think we need to stop finding ourselves in a situation like this where one or another is barely hanging to life. This reminds me too much of the time the bomb went off when I was escaping Michael. Only this time, Raphael is on his back, his kind yellow eyes closed. He looks ashen, and I have to stifle a sob. Dropping on my knees before I even reach him, I crawl to his side.

"His chest is not moving." Colt and Beelzebub are kneeling across from me, so I look at them. "Why is his chest not moving?"

'He is alive, Helena," Colt says somberly, as if that will make me calm down.

"I don't give a shit, Colt. Make his chest move, like now." I might sound hysterical, but that's fine, because I am.

"Hel." Eric crouches next to me, reaching for me, but I swat his hands away. "They already gave him more than he should have from their energy. Love, he is an Archangel, he can't have too much energy fed into him from Hell."

"Bullshit. There was nothing wrong with him after they did that." I don't understand why the three of them are just sitting there. It's driving me insane. "Do it!" Yanking on Eric's hand, I place it on Raphael's chest. "Feed him those shadows of yours Eric, or so help me God I'll stab you."

"You can't make that choice for him, Hel. Believe me when I tell you I want nothing more than to heal him." Eric looks pained. "But we can't. It'll change who he is, what he is."

"What? It'll make him evil or something?" My stomach is flip flopping, but I refuse to give up.

"He won't eat humans." Eric tries a joke, but my glare shuts him up, and he sighs. "It'll put more darkness in him, Hel. I'm not sure he will want that."

"That's fine." All three look at me like I've grown horns. Maybe I have. "There is a piece of the Devil in all of us. I'm your living proof. Heal him now, Eric. We don't have much time." When they don't move right away, I want to scream. "All of you should've thought about this shit before you decided to join me on this suicide path. If Raphael dies, nothing is stopping the jinn from snatching someone else, and I'll be at the top of their list after that. They want Raphael for a reason, and I'll be damned if I let them have him, dead or alive. Now, heal him before I go nuclear again."

That works like someone just poked them in the ass. All three of them spring into action, their hands stretched out above the Archangel. I hold my breath, waiting for what feels like an eternity. I'm not sure my heart is beating. Just when I'm ready to go insane, Raphael gasps a long breath, his back bowing off the ground. The sound coming from me is something between a sob and a laugh. Eric, Beelzebub, and Colt drop on their backs, breathing heavily. I ignore them all when the golden gaze locks on mine.

"Raphael…" Okay fine, I'm crying like a little girl, but I don't care. "You are okay."

"It's really Helena, the jinn is dead," Beelzebub grumbles.

Raphael jumps up, hugging me like he hasn't seen me in years. I laugh and cry, my snot and tears smudging his blood-covered shirt.

"I'm sorry." Sniffing, I keep repeating it. "I'm sorry. I'm so sorry…"

"You have nothing to be sorry about, Helena." Hearing Raphael's voice makes me ugly cry.

Bawling my eyes out, I clutch his arms. "You might grow horns now."

"What?" The question is half incredulous, half a burst of laughter.

The twins and Beelzebub release deep belly laughs and I really, really want to stab them right now. I don't, only because of something slamming into my back, sending both Raphael and I rolling in tangled limbs.

"Misstress…I ate his face…"

You guessed it. Narsi found us again.

Chapter Thirty-Three

HELENA

It took us most of the night to find the rest of the people scattered through Atlanta. It turns out, the jinn impersonating me was the chief honcho pulling the strings in this realm. Eric is beside himself from happiness because I won't have to infiltrate their ranks. I never knew he has that many teeth, and that he can smile so much. It's like his face is frozen in that state the last two days.

It's weird as hell.

More people start showing up at the safe house, and not just demons. Angels, even humans, start popping up on the street, waiting until we let them through the wards. We need to look for a bigger place soon since we are being packed like sardines at the moment.

"I'll be back as soon as I can," Eric tells me, pecking me on the lips before he disappears through the front door of the building.

Him, Beelzebub and Leviathan are going to Hell. Mammon turns out to be as slippery as a snake. He follows us here from Hell, making as much damage as he can, but as soon as the demons start dying and the jinn are gone, he bolted right back to his realm, thinking he is safe. I don't know about Beelzebub and Eric, but if the look on Leviathan's face is any indication, I would be petrified if I was Mammon. They'll also try to get the other fallen to join our fight.

The portals are still unstable, opening up all over the place. George and Cass found some of the hunters and brought them into our fold. Now all of them, along with Maddison's ever-growing army of demons, are patrolling the area and forcing whatever comes through the portals back. It doesn't matter if it's coming from Hell or from Heaven. The damn jinn are everywhere, and until we know for sure they are gone to their own realm, we will not let anyone get by us.

"I think I'm ready." Raphael stops next to me where I'm leaning on the doorframe.

"I'm not sure this is a good idea." My fingers wrap around his forearm.

I started touching him the last two days, as if reassuring myself that it's really him and I'm not imagining it. He scared the shit out of me when I thought he was going to die. Many have been killed because of me, but like hell I'll carry an Archangel on my conscious. He will stay alive if I have to force him.

A giggle bursts from me, and he looks at me with his golden eyes.

"What's funny?" Maddison comes from down the hall, looking from the Archangel to me.

"I was just thinking how much Raphael scared me and that I'd force him to stay alive if I had to." I grin at him when he laughs.

"I have every intention to be alive." He pets my hand

that's gripping his forearm. "I promised your mother, and I will keep my vow. Although I'm not sure anymore who is protecting whom."

"There'll be plenty of time for you to protect her, Archangel. I have a feeling this was not the worse that we will face." Maddison looks too serious for my liking.

"Why? We have more trouble?" The Archangel's face turns stormy and dark, his golden eyes darkening.

My stomach drops to the floor at that. Ever since I kind of forced the twins and Beelzebub to heal him, he is easier to anger, and there is this cloud of danger surrounding him even when he is relaxed. I don't want to think too hard about it because it'll drive me insane. I keep telling myself that Raphael is just too kind and too soft. Nothing can make him bad. Right? You must have evil in you for something to bring it to the surface.

There is a piece of the Devil in all of us. My own words ring in my head, the ones I said so they can heal him. But Raphael is...well, Raphael. Still kind, still smiling. Only he has an edge to him now. I'm not sure if that's a good or a bad thing. Only time will tell.

"Nothing for you to worry about." Maddison waves off his concerns. "Go do what you need to do and let's hope we can be prepared for whatever comes next."

"I will not be long, Helena." Raphael offers me a tight smile before leaving through the door.

"You think any of them will agree to join us and help?" I don't look at Maddison, keeping my eyes on Raphael's retreating back.

"We have nothing to lose by offering a chance to join." She leans her shoulder opposite me, watching the Archangel too. "They'll either agree, or they won't."

Raphael is going back to Heaven. He wants to find

Gabriel and try to convince him to join forces with us. According to him, in a loud debate—I don't want to call it screaming at each other—he had with the twins and the fallen, the angels will agree to fight together so we can get rid of the jinn. I'm skeptical, but that's because of my own trauma from the jinn impersonating Michael.

"So, what's with you and Leviathan?"

Maddison startles at my question, and her high cheekbones get tainted with red. My mouth hangs open from such a normal reaction coming from the always-poised woman. Her thick lashes cover her too-blue eyes for a long moment. I realize she's collecting herself so she can answer. It makes me feel bad that I just blurted out the question like it's any of my business what is going on in her life. But I really like Maddison, and her next to Leviathan? That's too much perfection and hotness in one place I'll tell you that much. My eyes hurt from all that beauty when they stand next to each other. Plus, the dragon boy is way too protective when it comes to Eric's cousin.

"It's a long story that I would like to leave in the past if you don't mind." She smiles, but her eyes look sad. My heart clenches.

"Sorry, I didn't mean to pry." And because I'm me and I can't keep my mouth shut, I have to keep talking. "It just doesn't look like he wants to leave things in the past." Twisting my lips in a grimace, I groan. "Sorry, I'm shutting up now."

"It's fine." Her musical laughter bounces off the walls. "Don't worry about it."

"Mistress…" Narsi throws himself at my legs, jolting my knees.

"Easy there, buddy." Grabbing a handful of his hair, I

hold him still, or he will climb me like a koala. "I hope you didn't eat anyone's face."

Maddison laughs, but someone calls her name, and she walks away, leaving me with my sidekick. I can finally have that one day where I can just breathe and not fight for my life. I'm planning to enjoy it as much as I can. With everyone going to one place or another, I think what I'm going to do is just sit and blink. That's all the action my body is going to get until I have to move.

"I didn't..." the Trowe hisses, and he looks sad about it. I have no idea what I'm going to do with him.

"Great!" Sounding too cheery to my own ears, I turn around and drag him by his hair along with me. It's the only way to keep him still, or he will run up and down the hall-way. "Let's feed you some real food and maybe you won't like faces anymore." He doesn't look like he thinks that will happen.

"Hel!" Eric's voice stops me in my tracks.

Releasing Narsi, I bolt out the door, my heart in my throat. Damn it, one damn day is all I wanted. What on earth happened now for him to be back before he even left. I feel Maddison rushing right behind me as well, so she must've heard him too.

Eric meets me at the bottom of the stairs. Judging by the look on his face, I can't tell if it's good news or bad. He looks happy but worried, pissed and excited, all at the same time. When we just stand there staring at each other, Maddison gets to the point as usual.

"Well?" she snaps at Eric, and he takes a deep breath.

I hold mine.

"We found Satanael." He grabs my hand, and it's a good thing because I'm about to faint. "We didn't get to the portal, but we scouted the warehouse one last time. None of us can convince him we are real, and he demands to see his daughter to believe us. He wants to see you," Eric tells me.

Oh my God!

That means I need to go to meet my father. It implies that I...I have to...to look the devil in the eye.

Shit! Holy shit!

vinci-books.com/devilintheeye

They say the Devil gives you everything you want. In my case? He gave me daddy issues.

Surviving Hell was one thing. Now dear old Dad—aka Satan— wants a family reunion, and it's not for tea and biscuits. With demons loose and Heaven and Hell actually agreeing (for once), I might be humanity's last hope… or its biggest mistake. No pressure, right?

Turn the page for a free preview…

To Look the Devil in the Eye: Chapter One

HELENA

"She keeps hiding from me." Eric's frustrated growl carries through the hallway. "That woman will be the death of me. You'd think..." his words trail off along with the fading footsteps.

Blowing a breath through pursed lips, I sag against the wall, sliding down until my butt hits the floor. Okay, so I have been hiding. If he didn't keep pushing me to meet with Satanael, it wouldn't have been necessary, but he is as stubborn as I am. So, this is what we do now. Eric walks around the half-destroyed building where we've set up camp looking for me, and I run around, doing my best to avoid him.

I've jumped through a portal landing in Hell on a whim. I stood in front of Lucifer telling him to pull the stick out of his ass. I even jumped on the back of a dragon from Hell and fought against jinn. But the moment my father was mentioned, I turned into a blubbering idiot and ran.

And I'm not feeling bad about it either. Hell, no. It's so not happening.

"If you don't turn that judgmental mug away from me, I'm going to stab you, Narsi." Tracking my sidekick from the corner of my eye, I don't miss the deranged grin he sends my way.

"Satanael knows many secrets, mistress." Hissing, he crawls on all fours towards me. "It will be wise to hear his words."

"You know what's also wise?" Turning to glare at him stops him from moving closer. "To keep your mouth shut instead of lecturing me."

"Your father…"

"Hector is my father!" Snapping at him, my shoulders hunch with the anger hearing the damn word father associated with Satan brings me.

"The human has no idea what you are or what you need." Lifting on his feet for the first time, the Trowe grows a backbone for the first time when it comes to me. "You need to hear Satanael's words more than he needs to speak them."

"And you know this how?" Narrowing my eyes, I watch the Trowe squirm. "What is it that you haven't told me?"

"You have a great responsibility, mistress." Dropping on his hands and knees again, he cocks his head like a bird. "I was bound not to speak your truth, but Satanael can tell you everything."

Closing my eyes, I thump my head on the wall in frustration. Everything in me rebels at the idea of facing Satanael. At the same time, guilt eats a hole in my stomach at knowing he is still trapped in that warehouse, waiting to see his daughter.

After the first day of not letting anyone near him until he saw me, he stopped being stupid and agreed to be freed.

Eric got back a few hours later with burns all over his arms, his skin blistering and cracking as blood dripped in a trail behind him where he walked. He was so angry at me that day, even refusing help from his brother and the other two Fallen. All of them tried, but whatever was holding Satanael trapped was not easily removed. Maddison suggested she would give it a go, but Leviathan went a little nuts. Okay, he shifted into a dragon and started spitting fire all over the place, so that went out the window fast.

Now all of us are upset with each other, and avoidance is the theme of the week. All because I'm a coward.

Narsi perks up, stretching his neck and tilting his head left and right. Watching the Trowe is like seeing a car wreck. Horrible to look at, but no matter how hard you try, you simply can't pull your eyes away. You just stand there, horrified and fascinated at the same time.

"The hunters are back." His lips stretch into a terrible smile, too wide for his tiny face.

"Wha…" It takes me a second to comprehend what he said, but the moment understanding hits me, I scramble to my feet. "Let's go."

George and Cass have been gone for a few days. I refuse to think about them, too afraid that they'll meet their end if crossing paths with Mammon and his lackeys. Knowing that they are back is like a fog being lifted from my head. Forgetting that I'm still hiding from my mate, I rip the door open and bolt out of the room I've used for hiding. Colliding with a hard body, the air is pushed out of my lungs with a very loud *oomph*, ending up on my ass on the floor.

Narsi snickers.

"There you are." Eric reaches for me, pulling me to my feet.

"Oh." Giggling nervously, I slap his hands away. "Hey, monster boy. I didn't see you standing there."

"Which is the only reason that you are actually standing here with me." Clenching his fists, a muscle jumps in his jaw.

"I have no idea what you are talking about." Lifting my chin up, I stare him down.

"Really?" With a voice dry as a desert, Eric arches an eyebrow at me.

Narsi decides to burst into a fit of giggles at that exact moment, and we both turn to glare at him. Instead of cowering away, the crazy bugger starts jumping around, wiggling his body like he is trying to shake off flees. The giggles are high pitched, a sound that taunts me.

"I think he is going insane." Frowning, I watch my sidekick completely losing it in the hallway.

"She does not fear you, Shadow." Narsi keeps giggling, turning in circles like a dog chasing its tail. "No, she does not."

"He does have a point." Still watching the crazy show, I can't help but grin at Eric.

"You and this damn Haltija are a disaster waiting to happen." He growls the words but can't hide the corners of his lips twitching in a barely contained smile.

"He said George and Cass are back." Turning away from Narsi, I start down the hallway. "I need to see if everything is okay and if they brought someone back."

"You mean Hector?" Falling in step with me, I feel Eric's arm brushing mine.

It sends a pleasant shiver down my spine. The man is too hot for my sanity, and I'm not sure how much longer I can keep avoiding him. I miss his arms around me and his full lips on mine, but all that disappears the second I remember that he will start talking about Satanael.

"I do want to see Hector. To know that he is alive..." With a deep sigh, I rub my forehead, the building headache already pounding at my temples. "But I'll take anything at this point. As long as we get to save and protect some of them."

"Hel..." His warm, calloused fingers wrap around my arm, stopping me as he turns me to face him. "You can't keep taking responsibility for every life lost in this situation. All of us feel guilty that we should've seen it coming, but you...you let all of it tear at your heart like you are the one that caused all of this."

"It was me, Eric." My voice packs a lot of heat when I yank my arm away from him. "Or did you forget how all of this started? I will not shy away from my part in it. Everyone has every right to hate me and want me dead." The ground under our feet groans and shudders, forcing us both to stumble away from each other.

"Deep breaths, cupcake." Eric's voice is strained, even when he tries to lighten up the moment with that stupid nickname. "We will talk about all that later. I was coming to get you." When my eyes turn to slits, he smirks at me. "I knew where you were. I just figured you'd come to your senses and come out on your own."

"You and Shadow have a soul bond, mistress," Narsi hisses next to me, and I nudge him away with my boot. "He can sense you when he is close, yes he can." Grinning that deranged smile, he looks from me to Eric.

"Tell me again why I keep him around?" The headache is getting worse.

"Because it's who you are, Helena." Threading his fingers through mine, Eric moves us along the hallway. "It's what I love and hate about you. You will stick your neck out for anyone, even those that don't deserve it. Although"—Glancing at the Trowe over his shoulder, he smiles, his handsome face lighting up with it—"the Haltija is useful, I must admit."

"You say that because he tries to bite Colt every time you get frustrated with your brother." Snorting, I shake my head, remembering Colt shouting for me to call off Narsi when he sneaked up in his room while he was sleeping and almost bit off half of his face. "The two of you act like two-year-old's."

"My brother will live." Grinning like a fool, he winks at me and my knees almost buckle. "It's a good thing we heal fast."

"Right." Shaking off the slack jaw and subtly wiping the little bit of drool from the corner of my mouth, I stare straight ahead.

I need to corner him somewhere, have my way with him, and then run before he opens his mouth to talk. That way, I won't listen to lectures, and I'll stop acting like I'm deprived. You might think that heat that burns in your veins when you start a relationship will eventually fade. That it'll become more bearable, so you can actually look at your other half without wanting to jump his bones. In our case, instead of fading away, it only burns hotter by the day. I can't even look at Eric without getting all hot and bothered, and his smoldering gaze tells me he feels the same. Even when we are ready to punch each other in the face.

Seeing the front doors of the building pulls me away from my hormonal insanity. The first thing I notice is Beelzebub's broad back blocking the doorway. Releasing Eric's hand, my feet speed up. Pushing the large Fallen is out of the question, so I squeeze through what little opening is left between him and the doorframe, screeching to a halt on top of the steps.

"What on earth is going on here?" My shout turns everyone's attention to me.

"I'll eat their face!" Narsi hisses next to me.

To Look the Devil in the Eye:
Chapter Two

"I will not stay here with demons!" a hunter I've seen around Sanctuary snaps, getting in George's face. I don't remember his name, but I never liked him; I know that much.

"Narsi, get your ass inside. You're not eating anyone." Grabbing the Trowe's hair, I hold him back, turning to Beelzebub. "Can you please lock him inside somewhere? He will only mess up this situation more than it already is."

"Look at her!" The jerk has spittle flying out of his mouth, his face turning red in anger. "You want us to become like her? Turn our back on Heaven? All your souls will burn in Hell for eternity."

"How melodramatic." I'm debating if letting Narsi loose will shut the idiot up. My headache is turning my vision blurry, and the loud yelling is not helping at all. "Unless you were hiding under a rock, you should know this has nothing to do with Heaven, or Hell for that matter."

About twenty or so hunters, all worse for wear with dirty uniforms and smudges of dirt and dried blood all over them, are huddled in one corner at the front of the building, eyeing me warily. Until recently, these were faces I've seen daily, and now those faces are eyeing me with suspicion that twists my stomach into knots. What's making it even more painful for me is that it reminds me of how I looked at Eric and Maddison when they were only trying to save my life. Giving Beelzebub an apologetic glance, I'm graced with an understanding smile on the Fallen's face.

"Talk to them." Taking Narsi by the scruff of his neck, Beelzebub urges me further into the front yard with a plate-sized hand on my back. "They are scared and confused. We don't know what they've seen or been through until your friends found them." Glancing at Eric, the corner of his mouth twists in displeasure. "And tell your mate to stop glaring at them. It's not going to help."

"You want them here?" I have no idea why I'm surprised by the large man at this point. He looks scary as hell with his size and red eyes, but so far, only understanding and support is what I've received from him.

"We can use all the help we can get, Helena." Turning away, he lifts the Trowe in the air and carries him kicking and wiggling inside.

Eric comes closer to my side, and I elbow him in the ribs. "Stop glaring at them."

"I don't like the way they are looking at you."

If there is one thing I know about, Eric, it's that no matter what is going on, if he sees someone even looking at me sideways he will stop to glare or punch them in the face for it, no matter if the world is ending or not. It's heart-warming and annoying at the same time.

"You don't have to like it." Moving closer to where Cass is doing a face-off with the hunters, her hands on her hips, my lips pucker and blow out a breath. "Just don't growl at them."

"I don't growl." The words are growly, and when I turn to pointedly look at his face, his lips flatten in a thin line. "I'll try."

Chuckling at his words, I stride next to my friends with my shoulders squared.

"I'm so happy you made it back safe." Reaching George, I give him a hug, his familiar scent and warmth calming my nerves.

His arms wrap around me, tightening like bands, and I feel his stiff body relax after a moment. I guess we both needed that—the comfort of a family—because that's exactly what we were to each other most of our lives. To my surprise, Eric grabs forearms with my friend, slapping his back. George nods once firmly, holding onto my mate's arm longer than necessary. That's when I notice how tired and worried he looks.

"You didn't come across any trouble, did you?" Half of my question gets muffled in Cass's hair when she almost tackles me to give me a hug.

"There is nothing left of the Order." My heart does a painful thump at the troubled look on George's face. "They are the only ones we could find. And we found them in the forest around Sanctuary when a few of them tried to attack us."

"Nothing is left because of the demons you want us to join," the jerk snarls from behind George.

"Listen to me, asshole." Pushing away from my friend, I get right up in the hunter's face. "No one will force you to stay here. All of us are fighting the demons that are trying to destroy Earth. If you think you have a better chance of doing it on your own, go right ahead. Get the hell out of here."

"No one in this place is going to hurt you. We are trying to keep you safe." With each word, I take a step closer to him, forcing him to step back. "When my life was on the line, I didn't see any of you stepping up to protect me. Unlike you, my soul—the one that will burn for eternity according to you—will not let me turn my back on you. I guess that makes me the biggest of evils you've ever seen."

"You are an abomination." The hunter finds his voice, his shoulders curving inwards. "You opened the portal to Hell and brought this on our heads." Glancing over my shoulder, his face pales, and he stumbles back.

"Eric." Groaning, I rub my face. I don't have to turn to see him. Nothing can freak out a hunter more than a pissed off demon.

"I did not growl."

A humorless laugh bursts from me at his snapped words. My gaze flicks to Cass, and I can see she's barely hiding her own smile.

"Listen." Ignoring Eric, I look from face to face in the group of hunters. "Yes, I'm an abomination. No wishing or praying can change what I am. But I mean you no harm. This place"—Flinging a hand, I point at the building behind us—"is protected by wards. Nothing can hurt you here. It's a safe house...as safe as we can make it. Come inside. Eat, rest. And when you've seen for yourself, you can decide what you want to do. Nothing and no one will hold you here against your will. We are trying to fight against those that attacked the human realm. You can join us or stay and wait. We expect nothing from you. I just don't want you to die."

"And that is enough convincing. Now, you can do what

you want." George grabs me by my shoulder and pulls me away from where I am facing the group. "I brought you here. It's up to you if you want to stay." Pushing me towards Eric, he grabs Cass by the arm and drags her with him. "I, on the other hand, am hungry and tired. I'm going inside."

Eric doesn't wait for more encouragement. As soon as I'm close enough to reach, he flings me in his arms, his long legs eating up the space to the open door within a second. Craning my neck, I see the hunters over his shoulder looking at each other. One by one, they gingerly move and follow us inside. I open my mouth to tell George, who is right on Eric's heels, that they are coming, but he shakes his head, shutting me up. A weight is lifted off my chest when all of them, including the jerk, enter the wards. He can hate me and be angry all he wants as long as they stay alive. I don't want Mammon or the jinn to take more lives than they already have.

My head rests on my mate's shoulder as I sigh. One disaster averted. Soon I'll have to sneak around again when Eric starts talking about Satanael. Another groan passes my lips at that thought. The hunters were freaking out about me being just an abomination. What will they do when they hear I'm Satan's daughter?

Grab your copy…
vinci-books.com/devilintheeye

About the Author

Maya Daniels, USA Today Bestselling and multi-award-winning supernatural suspense author, is a fun-loving woman with many talents.

She traveled the world, gaining life experiences that helped her career as an investigative journalist, as well as her storytelling. Maya writes compelling tales of magic, mythical creatures, loyalty, and life-changing friendships with snarky female characters—much like herself.

Her travels have taken her to Europe, Africa, Asia, Australia, and America. Born with her feet in motion, she currently resides in Ohio, spinning her next epic story that you will not want to put down.

Her biggest 'sins' are her love of chocolate and coffee—through an IV drip! One to never sit still, Maya practices Reiki healing, different types of martial arts, reads about the arcane, talks to furry creatures more than humans, picks up a sledgehammer for home improvement, and travels with her fated mate, seeking her own adventures.

9 781036 706623